W9-DHR-938

WonderTales
from
Around the World

WONDER TALES

from AROUND *the* WORLD

HEATHER FOREST

Illustrations by David Boston

August House Publishers, Inc.
LITTLE ROCK

Printed in the United States of America

10 9 8 7 6 5 4 3 2 1   HB
10 9 8 7 6 5 4 3 2 1   PB

LIBRARY OF CONGRESS CATALOGUING-IN-PUBLICATION DATA
Forest, Heather
Wonder tales from around the world / retold by Heather Forest ;
illustrations by David Boston.
p.   cm.
Summary: Includes twenty-seven folktales from Europe,
Asia, Africa, India, the Arctic, and the Americas.
ISBN 0-87483-421-X (hb : alk. paper). —
ISBN 0-87483-422-8 (pb : alk. paper)
1. Tales. [1. Folklore.] I. Boston, David, ill. II. Title.
PZ8.1.F76Wp 1995
[398.2]—dc20   95-20459

Executive editor: Liz Parkhurst
Project editor: Rufus Griscom
Design director: Ted Parkhurst
Cover art: David Boston
Cover Design: Harvill Ross Studios, Ltd.

The paper used in this publication meets the minimum requirements of
the American National Standard for Information Sciences—Permanence of
Paper for Printed Library Materials, ANSI Z39.48-1984.

AUGUST HOUSE, INC.   PUBLISHERS   LITTLE ROCK

A Dedication

398.2

I've traveled around the world
without leaving home.
I've been anywhere
my imagination wants to roam.
I take a look,
in a folktale book,
and travel on the wings of words.

Soaring to faraway places,
ancient times,
or magical spaces,
I find a fantasy view ...
reading a book
from the library shelf
marked
398.2.

Contents

▲▲▲▲▲▲▲▲▲

Introduction

▲▲▲▲▲▲▲▲▲▲▲▲

*S*ince ancient times, wonder tales have been a part of the vast oral tradition of cultures around the world. These non-realistic folktales have a magical, "long ago and far away" quality. A wonder tale invites the listener to suspend the logic of ordinary reality and leap into an imaginative world where impossible events can occur. In fantasy, we do not have to walk on solid ground ... we can soar.

The multicultural stories in this folktale collection, which I have retold in prose with a touch of original poetry, have in common a delightful, fanciful spirit. Their broad, colorful characters and metaphorical, fantasy-filled plots may strike resonant chords and remind readers of parts of themselves, their lives, or of others they know. Polished by the tongues of tellers over centuries, these imaginative folktales are a distillation of human experience, preserved and passed on in an entertaining form.

The folktale plots selected and retold for this anthology have a global perspective, including wonder tales from Europe, Asia, Africa, India, the Arctic, and the Americas. Yet a striking similarity of human hopes, fears, and dreams shines through. In tales from places far and wide, good overcomes evil, justice prevails, generosity is rewarded, and love has power over discord. The wise, the foolish, the cruel, and the kind are colorful threads in this ancient tapestry of tales.

As a professional storyteller since 1974, I perform stories for listeners of all ages in theaters, schools, and storytelling festivals throughout the United States. My minstrel performance style of storytelling interweaves original poetry, guitar, and the sung and spoken word. I enjoy the musical sound of words. I wrote this folktale book to be read by older youths and adults, but I composed the language so that the tales could be fluidly read outloud to younger people.

As a storyteller, I seek to retell old tales in vivid, efficient phrasing, with words that are pleasing to the ear. Here are some simple suggestions for those who want to bring these stories to life by reading them outloud. Clearly picture the tale in your imagination as it is being read. Watch the tale as if it were a movie behind your eyes, and allow those colorful interior images to permeate your face and voice as you read. By bringing the tale to life within yourself, the dialogue and narration can come to life for others too, as the story is told.

I invite you to cultivate your imagination with these wonder-filled tales.

HEATHER FOREST
HUNTINGTON, NEW YORK

The Magic Brocade

A FOLKTALE FROM CHINA

There once was a weaver who filled her fine silk brocades with flowers and birds that seemed so real they almost quivered. She and her three sons never went hungry, for when she brought her wares to the marketplace everyone would gasp at their beauty and grasp for their purses.

One day, after she had sold all her brocades, she walked past the stalls in the marketplace with her pocket full of money. Her eye was suddenly caught by a small painting half-hidden behind other wares. She picked up the painting to admire it more closely. Her eyes traveled over the tiny image of a fine white house surrounded by fields of red flowers. A crystal pool shimmered in the sunlight beside the house, and the dancing fish seemed so lifelike they almost moved. A lazy river wound its way about the edges of the field. Cattle and sheep grazed peacefully. She could almost feel the painting's warm sunlight on her face. How she longed to be in such a place! Without considering for even a moment, she reached into her pocket and spent all of her hard-earned money on the precious painting. Smiling, she set off for home with the treasure pressed to her heart under her jacket.

Her three sons greeted her when she arrived at her humble thatched cottage at the foot of the mountains. "How was your luck today, Mother?" inquired the eldest.

"I had great luck," she answered with a grin.

"Then have you bought us special foods to eat?" asked the second son, licking his lips at the thought of expensive sweets.

"I have brought you a feast for your eyes," she said, drawing forth the tiny

painting from her jacket.

Her two older sons grumbled their disappointment. But her youngest, delighting in his mother's pleasure, gazed at the painting and said, "It is an exquisite picture."

"Oh, if we could only live in such a place," the weaver sighed.

Her two older sons muttered, "Stop dreaming! We could never afford to live in such a place."

Her youngest son saw the shadow of sadness pass over the weaver's face. He said, "Mother, make a brocade that looks like this painting. While you work, it will be as though you are there beside the shimmering pond."

The weaver set about instantly to weave the image of the tiny painting. She immersed herself in the image, and so great was her joy that she worked without stopping.

She used the finest threads of silver and gold. She wove all day, each day, and at night she burned pine branches to make enough light to weave longer. She wove only this picture and soon had nothing to take to market.

"Make something that you can quickly sell at the market or we will have to cut firewood to earn some money," complained the two older brothers. "You are wasting too much time on this brocade!"

But the weaver could not stop her wonderful brocade. The youngest son calmed his two brothers and said, "Do not fret. I will cut the wood we need so that Mother can finish her brocade."

The weaver wove for one year without stopping, and her eyes began to water as she worked. She wove her tears into the crystal waters of the pond. After another year her eyes began to shed tears of blood, and these tears she wove into the red flowers swaying in the fields. At the end of the third year the weaver was almost blind but the brocade was done. The sun hung like a red plum in the sky and the house stood white and welcoming. Cattle and sheep grazed in fields of graceful grasses.

She brought her work outside to admire it in the sunlight. Suddenly, a great wind came and whisked it out of her hands. She shrieked with alarm as the brocade swept high above her head and flew off toward the East. Her grief was beyond measure, and she fell to the earth in a faint.

Her sons carried her into the house and laid her on the bed. "Mother!" they cried, "what can we do?"

When at last she opened her eyes she said to her sons, "Please find my brocade or I will surely die."

The oldest son set off first, walking toward the East. After a while he came upon a white-haired woman sitting in front of a stone house. Beside her was a stone horse, its neck stretched out as if to eat the red berries on a bush.

"Good day, old woman," said the boy. "Have you seen a brocade fly by?"

"Indeed I have!" said the old woman, "And I know all about it, too! The fairies of Sun Mountain have stolen it from your mother. They have flown it away to copy it, for it is far more beautiful than anything they have ever made. You can get it back for your mother, but there are several things that you must do. First, knock out your two front teeth. I will put them in this toothless horse's mouth. He will come to life and carry you to Sun Mountain. The journey will be difficult. He will carry you across Fire Mountain and although the flames will lick you like cats, you must not complain of the heat. He will carry you across an icy sea and, although the cold ocean spray will pierce your face like needles, you must not utter a sound. Once you have arrived at Sun Mountain the fairies will give you back the brocade."

The boy's face paled at the thought of knocking out his teeth.

"Well," said the old woman, noticing his hesitation, "I see that this is more than you are willing to do. So take this box of gold to your family, as a gift from the fairies, and live well."

The oldest son took the gold and headed for home. When he arrived at the crossroads, he thought, "If I bring all this gold home I must share it four ways. If I keep it for myself I will never have to work!" And he turned toward the city and did not come home.

Two months passed. The weaver grew weaker with each passing day. She begged her second oldest son to go forth and find her brocade. He set out toward the East and when he met the old white-haired woman, he too, refused to make the journey to Sun Mountain. She gave him a box of gold from the fairies and he headed home. Like his older brother, the second son decided to keep the gold for himself and set off for the city.

Meanwhile, at the cottage, the weaver grew paler and paler. She cried so often she could barely see.

"I will find your brocade," said the youngest son, "since I cannot bear your sorrow any longer."

He walked East and at last he arrived at the stone house. The old woman smiled and said, "I suppose you are looking for a brocade that has flown by this way."

"Yes, I am!" said the boy. "I would do anything to find it."

"Perhaps and perhaps not," said the old woman, and she carefully explained the tasks that he must perform.

Without hesitation, the boy knocked out his two front teeth. In an instant they were in the horse's mouth, and the boy mounted the huge steed, who shuddered from stone to flesh and pawed the ground. The horse ate the red berries and galloped in a cloud of dust over the hills and valleys. Suddenly the boy felt a scorching heat on his skin. His hot face flushed red from the glowing flames of Fire Mountain as he traveled over its top. He gripped the reins and continued on. He galloped over the icy sea, shivering and shuddering as frigid water splashed and froze on his back. His tears became icicles and pierced his cheeks, but he did not utter a complaint.

At last, they came to Sun Mountain, where warmth and light drenched the sky. The horse slowed to a walk and stepped onto the shore. Before them was a fine palace with towers and banners and gardens all around. The boy jumped off the horse and entered the central hall of the palace. There he saw the fairy women sitting in a great circle about his mother's brocade. It was hung on an easel and all the fairies were busy making brocades just like it. The boy entered, bowed low and said, "Please, I have come for the brocade my mother made with her heart, hands, blood, and tears. If I do not return it to her, she will surely die."

The fairies all nodded and said, "You may have it back when we are finished copying it."

To make the work go faster, the fairies hung a huge pearl overhead. The pearl shed a luminous glow and the fairies worked through the night while the boy slept on the floor, waiting. At last all the fairies had gone to sleep, except for one beautiful sprite in red. She sighed with dismay as she looked at her own copy of the brocade. "My copy does not compare to the original. What a beautiful place. I wish I could live there." Since no one was looking, she embroidered a tiny picture of herself in the original brocade, and went to sleep.

Just then the boy woke up and, quick as a blink, he grabbed the brocade and ran. He leaped onto the horse's back and in a flash they were back at the stone house. The white-haired woman took the two front teeth from the horse and put them back in the boy's mouth. Then, for his bravery, she gave the boy a pair of magic deerskin shoes. With one step and a wish he was back at his mother's door.

"Mother! Mother!" he cried. "Get up and see! I have the brocade!"

The weaver lifted her head from her pillow and a smile spread over her face as she rose to greet her son. She blinked away the tears and clearly saw the brocade.

"Let's take it out into the sunlight!" she said, barely able to contain her joy.

She spread the brocade on the ground and was admiring it when suddenly it began to move. It floated upright and began to quiver and expand until it became the world around. The weaver gasped in amazement. There before her was a great grassy field of red flowers, a shimmering pond, a lazy winding river, and the fine white house. She and her son stepped into the field and were walking toward the white house when they saw a beautiful young woman dressed all in red coming toward them. It was the fairy who had sewn herself into the brocade.

The weaver's son married the woman in red and they all lived in great happiness in the white house, enjoying the bounty and beauty of their surroundings for many, many years.

ONE SPRING DAY, two old, ragged beggars came along. They were the two brothers who had squandered their wealth in the city. Seeing the fine white house, they plotted to steal from its owner. As they crept across the field, they saw their own mother, now white-haired with age, walking in the garden with their younger brother and a beautiful woman in red. Their cheeks flushed with embarrassment. Ashamed to face them, the brothers slunk away down the road and never troubled their door again.

The Talking Skull

There was once a man who was walking in search of food. He came upon a whitened skull lying on the ground in the hot sunlight. He approached the skull and wondered out loud, "What brought you here?"

The skull's jaw began to creak and move. The curious man moved closer to the skull and heard it say,

> *"Woe is me. Misery!*
> *I cannot shed a tear.*
> *Woe is me. Misery!*
> *My mouth has brought me here."*

The man was amazed! "A talking skull!" he exclaimed. He almost forgot his hunger for a moment. He was curious and asked, "How could your mouth bring you here?"

Then the skull spoke again and said, "I will show you. First, walk a distance in the direction that my nose points and you will find some calabashes filled with millet to eat."

The man walked and walked and came to some calabashes filled with grain. He was so happy to find food. He ran back to the skull and said, "Thank you! If I had not found these calabashes, I too might be a skeleton soon!"

The skull replied, "Do not tell anyone about me or you will be sorry."

The man ran to the village. He showed the food. Everyone was glad to see the grain. The King commanded that the man come to his hut. "Where did you find this food?" he asked.

Forgetting the warning of the skull, the man said, "A talking skull told me where to find the calabashes filled with millet."

"You are lying," said the King. "Perhaps you have stolen this food. There cannot be a talking skull."

"I will take you to it," boasted the man. "Then you will see that what I say is true."

"If you are lying we will cut off your head," said the King.

The man led the King and several warriors to the place where he had seen the skull. "There it is," he said.

The skull's dark eye sockets stared like small caves. Its jaw hung open. The man leaned close to the skull and said, "Now tell everyone where to find the food."

The skull sat white and silent in the sun.

"Please," said the man, a bit nervous under the glare of the King's eyes, "tell everyone what you told me!"

But the skull sat like a hard dry stone.

The man threw himself on the ground and begged, "Show them I am not a liar! Tell them! Tell them! Where is the food?"

But the only sounds they heard were birds and insects.

The King was outraged and commanded, "Kill him. Cut off his head, for he has lied."

And they cut off the man's head and left him there.

In time two whitened skulls were lying next to each other on the ground in the hot sun. The first skull turned to the second and finally said,

"Woe is me! Misery!
What I said was true.
It was my mouth that brought me here, my friend.
Your mouth has brought you too!"

The Magic Mill

One snowy Christmas eve, a poor brother knocked on his rich brother's door. "What do you want?" a gruff voice said, as the door creaked open.

Hat in hand, the poor man humbly replied, "Dear brother, my wife and I have no food at our house for the holiday. Please be kind and give us something special to eat."

The rich brother grumbled, "Since it's the holiday season, I will give you a ham. Just promise me that you will do as I say."

"I will do as you ask," said the poor brother, taking the ham.

"Well then," said the rich brother, slamming the door, "go to the Devil and leave me alone!"

As the poor brother walked away with the ham under his arm, he said to himself, "A promise is a promise. I will go to the Devil just as my brother requested."

The poor brother walked hour after hour and finally came to a large house with bright lights shining from every window. An old man, whose beard hung to the ground, was chopping wood nearby.

The poor brother said, "Pardon me, old man, I am looking for the Devil. Can you help me find my way?"

"Well," said the old man, "you've come to the Devil's own house. But if you go inside with that ham under your arm, everyone will want it. Don't sell it or trade it unless you get the Magic Mill from behind the door. It's good for grinding one thing or another. Bring it to me and I'll show you how to use it."

The poor brother entered the house. Big and small sprites jumped all over him, begging for the ham. He would not sell or trade it except for the Mill from behind the door. The poor brother was so steadfast, the Devil finally traded the Mill.

"Well done!" said the bearded old man, when he saw the brother holding the Mill. "Now you must learn to use it carefully or your magic will be your misfortune. When you want something, picture it in your mind and say, '*Magic Mill, Grind and Spill!*' To make it stop just say, '*Magic Mill, I've Had My Fill!*' "

"Thank you and goodbye!" said the poor brother. He hurried home to his wife with the treasure under his arm. When he entered his home his wife complained, "We've not two sticks to cross for fire under the porridge pot. What a sad Christmas this will be!"

"Not at all, dear wife," said her husband, putting the Mill on the table. He wished for a tablecloth and candles, and a moment later they appeared. Then a juicy roast, potatoes, and fine wine spread out before them with the help of the Mill. His wife clapped her hands with glee and asked, "Where did you get such a magical thing?"

But the man would not speak of it and she was too busy eating to question further. They ate their fill and then invited all the neighbors to a merry feast. Food and wine flowed from their table. Soon all the villagers heard of the party and people began arriving from every direction.

The rich brother saw a noisy crowd of villagers heading for his brother's house. Curious, he followed. When he saw the abundant food and wine, he burned with jealousy.

"How is it that just yesterday you came to me for a ham and now you feed the entire village a feast fit for a king? Where did you get all this food?" he asked his brother.

The poor brother smiled and said only, "From behind the door!"

Unsatisfied with this answer, the rich brother asked again and again. All this while, the poor brother was drinking wine, and it loosened his tongue. He finally told his rich brother about the Magic Mill.

"I must have it," said the rich brother. "I'll give you three hundred gold

pieces for the Mill."

The poor brother agreed to the sale. "But I must keep the Mill until haying time," he said. "By then, I will have wished a fortune from it."

At haying time, the rich brother came to claim the Mill. His brother carefully told him how to start the Mill. He did not tell him how to stop it.

The rich brother took the Mill home and announced to his wife, "Today, you will do the haying and I shall cook lunch for all the workers."

This amazed his wife since she'd never known him to cook before. "Very well," she said, eager to see what recipe he would prepare.

At noontime, the rich brother set the Mill on the table and imagined a fine lunch of porridge, herring, and bread. "*Magic Mill, Grind and Spill!*" he said. The Mill began to grind thick, tasty porridge. The finest herring and wheat bread spilled forth. The rich brother was delighted! The Mill kept grinding until porridge filled every bowl. Herring filled every plate. The bread piled high on the table. When there were no more bowls, porridge began spilling onto the floor. Herring floated everywhere. The brother waded about in the fishy mess, trying to stop the Mill. He turned it this way and that. But porridge, herring and bread kept spilling out until he had to open the parlor door so as not to drown in it. The mess filled the parlor to the window sills. He opened the front door and ran ahead of the huge wave of porridge and herring that followed him as he stumbled down the hill. Meanwhile, his wife and all the workers started home for lunch. Coming toward them was the fishy wave of porridge. Bumps and lumps of bread bobbed everywhere. "Start eating!" cried the rich brother, and ran to his brother's house.

"Turn off the Mill!" he begged, banging on his brother's door. "We will drown in herring and porridge!"

"I'll make it stop," said his brother slyly, "for another three hundred pieces of gold, and a promise that I can keep the Mill."

"Anything! Anything!" said the rich brother. "Just stop the mess!"

The poor brother commanded, "*Magic Mill, I've Had My Fill.*" It stopped and the poor brother got the Mill back. He wasted no time in wishing for more wealth than one could imagine. He built a huge house on the harbor

and had it plated with gold. Ships from far out at sea could see the shining roof. Many a sea captain stopped to visit the now wealthy man. They came to enjoy his hospitality or to sell him fine goods from faraway lands.

One day, the captain of a fishing boat came to call. The two men spoke of this and that and when the subject of the Magic Mill came about, the sea captain begged to see it. The brother brought the Mill down from the shelf and showed the sea captain the marvel.

The brother explained, "I just think of what I desire and say, '*Magic Mill, Grind and Spill.*' That's all there is to it! It grinds anything."

"But is it able to make salt?" asked the captain, "When I get a big catch, I need salt to preserve the fish until I can get them to market. What a joy it would be to have a Mill that could grind salt as I need it! I will give you one thousand pieces of gold for the Mill."

"It's not for sale," said the brother, ending the conversation. The sea captain bristled and left abruptly.

During the night, the sea captain crept back into the brother's house and stole the mill. He set sail immediately with the Mill on board. In the morning, far out at sea, the captain caught a net full of codfish. He put the Mill on the deck to make it grind. Imagining a mountain of salt, he said the magic words, "*Magic Mill, Grind and Spill,*" just as the brother had told him. To the sea captain's delight, salt began spilling from the mill. The salt piled up higher and higher on the deck. The ship began to list from side to side. "That's enough salt!" the sea captain said.

But the Mill kept grinding. The captain tried everything he could think of to stop the mill, but it kept on spilling salt! The brother had not mentioned anything about how to make the magic stop. The salt piled so high and heavy on the deck that the ship, the captain, and the Mill sank to the bottom of the sea.

To this day, somewhere at the bottom of the ocean, the Magic Mill is still grinding salt. And if you don't believe this story ... taste the sea water!

The Blizzard Witch of the North

A FOLKTALE FROM THE SIBERIAN ARCTIC

*W*hen Blizzard grips the land with her icy fingers, the far North is white with ice and snow. The dim light of winter can barely warm the frozen ground as the Sun drives a sled pulled by a reindeer with golden antlers across the sky. In the winter, the ride is short each day. Families huddle around the hearthfires in their deerskin *yarangas*.* If the fires go out, the thin skin of their houses is no protection against cold-hearted Blizzard.

One frigid winter day, as Blizzard walked the land around a Nenet village, a mother and her two children stayed snug and warm inside their house. The father had drowned while hunting seals the past spring, and the mother had to work very hard to tend the fire all alone. Her two children never helped her.

The mother was tired. As she lay down to rest, she said to her children, "I am sick. I can barely lift my head. Put some wood on the fire. Do not let the fire burn too low or the winter witch, Blizzard, will come into our house."

But the daughter combed her long black hair, braiding and loosening it endlessly. "I am too busy combing my hair, Mother," she said, "I cannot put any wood on the fire now. I will do it later."

"Son," said the mother, "come out from under your covers and tend the fire."

But the boy nestled under his deerskin blankets and said, "I will do it later, Mother. I am too tired to work now."

The fire began to burn lower and lower. Blizzard moved slowly across the

---
*dwellings

25

tundra with a great icy staff in her hand. Her snowy hair blew wildly around her long white robes. Her skin was frost and her teeth sparkled like icicles. She grinned wickedly as the fire dimmed in the *yaranga*.

"Please children," the mother said, "get up quickly and tend the fire! Do not let it go out. Heat and light are Blizzard's only fears."

But the girl combed her hair and the boy drew the blankets tightly around his shoulders and closed his eyes.

As the fire dimmed to just an ember, the door flap opened and in swirled Blizzard. The last spark of the fire flew into the air as Blizzard's blast of cold wind swept through the *yaranga*. The spark burned a tiny hole in Blizzard's white robe. In a fury she howled and reached for the children with icy fingernails. The mother rose up from her sleeping board and threw herself over the children. Blizzard struck the floor with her frozen staff and the mother turned into a giant sea gull. Her black-tipped wings covered the boy and girl, but it was no use. Blizzard wrapped herself around the bird and in a moment, both were gone in a flurry of ice and snow.

The son and daughter sat alone and shivering in the *yaranga* as they stared at the cold ashes in the hearth. "It's all your fault," said the girl. "If you had only done what Mother asked!"

"No," said the boy, "it's your fault! All you did was comb your hair!"

"Well, there's no sense in arguing about it now," said the girl.

"Yes, we must go and find our mother," said the boy, climbing out from under the blankets.

The children dressed in their warm parkas and tied snowshoes to their boots. The girl took a hunting knife and the boy took his father's bow and arrows. They tumbled out onto the snow and set off to find their mother.

Meanwhile, Blizzard had taken the giant sea gull to her ice palace on the tundra. She thumped her great staff on the ice floor and the sea gull turned back into the mother.

"Now you will repair the hole in my robe!" she howled.

The mother wept, thinking of her children alone in the *yaranga*. "Who will take care of them?" she worried, as she began to mend the hole in Blizzard's cold white robe with an ice needle.

But as the children traveled across the tundra, the Sun looked down from the sled in the sky and took pity on them. The Sun gave the boy three arrows of light to protect them on their way. The children thanked the Sun and continued across the icy land.

The world around them was white. Only small patches of lichen and moss poked through the snow. Suddenly a small deer bounded across their path. Its eyes were wide with fright.

"Look!" said the daughter. "A wolf is chasing the deer! It is coming this way!"

The son quickly took the first arrow of light and shot it at the wolf. The wolf turned and ran off. The children rushed to the trembling deer.

"Don't be frightened," said the girl, stroking its neck. "We are orphans, too. Come along with us."

The three travelers continued together, looking for their mothers. They walked and walked through the snow. Before long, they saw a dark form coming toward them. It was the mother deer. When she saw her fawn, she rushed to its side. The baby deer nudged the two children onto the mother deer's back. The mother deer quickly carried the two children across the ice and snow to Blizzard's palace.

A towering ice mountain stood before them. The children could see through the clear ice walls of the palace to where their mother was shivering and stitching Blizzard's snowy robe. Frozen tears covered her cheeks, and her aching fingers were blue with cold as she held the ice needle.

A deep canyon separated the children from the mountain. They wondered how they could ever cross the dark abyss to reach their suffering mother. The daughter lifted the hunting knife to her long black braid. Without hesitation, she cut off her beautiful treasure and made a long rope. The children tied a loop at one end and threw it across the gaping hole. It caught around a craggy outcropping of ice. They were just about to swing across when Blizzard called for her sister, Darkness, to blind them. Darkness descended the mountain and wrapped herself around the children so that they could not see. The boy felt for his bow and the second arrow of light. He shot it up to the sky. The arrow awakened the Sun's brothers, the Northern Lights. The rainbow giants crossed the sky, spreading a colorful pulsing glow across the night dome. The children could see and swiftly crossed the deep canyon on the black hair rope.

Blizzard moved menacingly across the ice to greet them. Her sharp icicle teeth sparkled and her snow hair swirled around her furious face. She howled and sent piercing winds to sting the children's cheeks. The son reached for the last arrow of light. The winds blew so hard against his small hands he could hardly aim. He summoned all of his courage and shot the arrow deep into the cold heart of Blizzard. With a sudden blast of harsh wind and a shriek, Blizzard whirled with fury until she could rage no more. The children clutched each other tightly. As Blizzard's howling disappeared, a soft snow fell and turned to rain. Winter melted away. The ice mountain vanished. Spring flower buds pushed up from the dark moist Earth everywhere. The air became warm and sweet.

The mother rushed to her children and gathered them in her arms. "I thought I would never see you again," she cried. "What brave hunters you have become."

Wiping the tears of joy, she hugged her son and daughter tightly and began to stroke their hair. "Daughter!" she exclaimed, "where is your beautiful braid?"

But before the daughter could answer, the mother saw the black shiny rope that had carried the children to her rescue.

"My hair will grow again," said the daughter with a radiant smile. "I am not sad to lose it, for now we have you back again."

Clinging to each other, they walked home to watch the Arctic spring bloom.

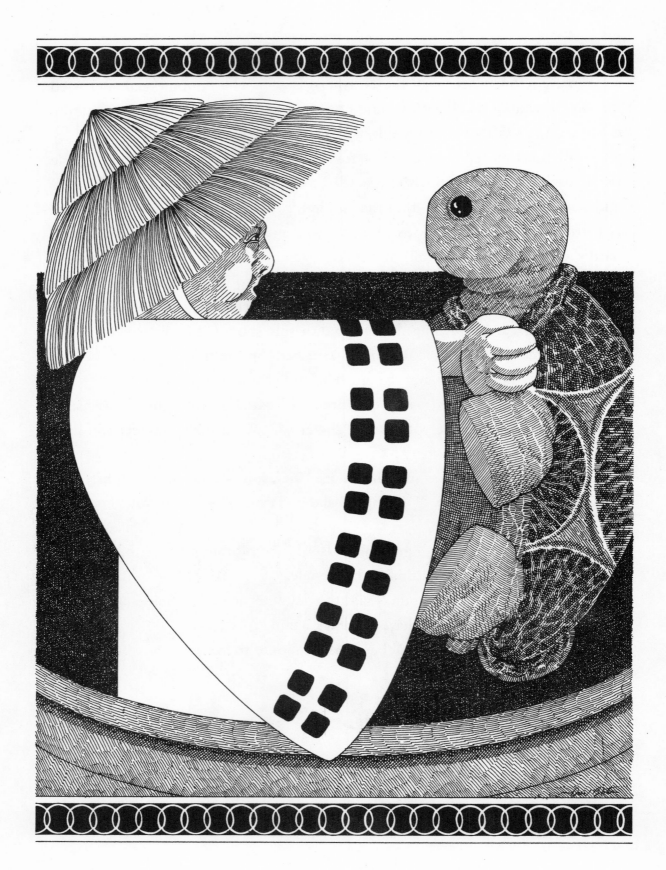

Urashima the Fisherman

A FOLKTALE FROM JAPAN

*L*eaving the tall, snow-capped mountains of Japan behind him, Urashima the fisherman rowed out to sea. He cast his nets, but caught no fish. The midday sun blazed overhead, and the gentle motion of his boat, bobbing on the waves, made him so drowsy he drifted to sleep. Suddenly, a splash awakened him. Tangled in his fishing net was a five-colored turtle struggling to free itself. Urashima felt pity for the creature and released it from the ropes. With a stretch and a yawn, he went back to his nap.

When he opened his eyes again, he beheld a delicate dark-haired woman seated beside him. Her gossamer gown sparkled in the sunlight. The scent of flowers and incense filled his nostrils.

"Do not be afraid," she said gently. "I am the daughter of the Dragon King of the Sea. Since you were so kind to the turtle, I have come to invite you to my palace."

Urashima could not take his eyes off her. He had never seen a more beautiful and mysterious woman. "I would be pleased to follow you anywhere," he finally said, finding his tongue.

"And would you love me as much as the shore loves the sea?" she asked, with a smile.

"Yes!" said Urashima.

"Would you love me as the stars love the night sky?" she asked, with a toss of her long black hair.

"Yes!" said Urashima, completely enraptured.

"Good!" she exclaimed, "then we shall go to the Island of the Immortals and live together in happiness forever."

They each took one oar and rowed far away from the snow-capped peaks of Japan. They rowed and rowed until they saw no land. The sea gulls flew above them, the sun set and rose. Still, they rowed.

At last they arrived at a distant shore. A jade palace loomed before them. Strange sea creatures and lovely handmaidens greeted them as they drew the boat to the beach. Giant sea horses escorted the couple, with great ceremony, to the Dragon King.

"Welcome," said the King, seated on a pearl-encrusted throne. "Make yourself at home here forever."

Delighted, Urashima bowed low and said, "I accept the invitation! I am happy to stay."

Servants brought forth a sumptuous feast of ten thousand flavors. Urashima tasted wine of every fruit. A wedding ceremony united the happy couple, who sat, arms entwined, until the sky became a rosy pink. As the night sky darkened, the handmaidens floated off to become stars. The sea creatures returned to the deep, and the couple was left alone to their bliss.

Days drifted into nights, and nights into days, like the tides. Urashima forgot his family and his home for a long time. One day, however, his father's face floated across his mind. His dear mother's face smiled at him. He saw her hand, longing to reach out and tenderly touch his shoulder.

"Oh, how I miss my parents!" Urashima suddenly said to his bride.

"Do not think about them," she warned, "or you will want to leave me."

"I cannot stop thinking of them. They float through my mind like a soft warm breeze. I wish only to visit them," he said. "I am happy here. I want to be with you. I promise that I will return."

There was no changing his mind. The maiden sighed and said, "Since you will not stay, I must give you this precious gift. Here is a lacquered box. Keep it close to you always and when you want to return, squeeze it hard."

She tied the box with a silver cord and, handing it to Urashima, she warned, "Do not open this box. If you betray my trust, then you will never see me again."

"It is a simple request," said Urashima, fingering the ornate black box with curiosity. "I will not open it."

The maiden walked with Urashima to the shore of the island. She dabbed her tears with a silk cloth as he climbed into the small boat that had brought them to this shore.

"Goodbye," he said, as he rowed away. "I will see you again soon."

Urashima rowed for days, and at last he saw the white snow-capped peaks of Japan piercing the sky. He rowed faster, for his heart was racing in anticipation of greeting his family again. As he came closer to the shoreline, he paused and looked with curiosity at the beach. It seemed different to him somehow, although he had docked his craft countless times before. He stepped out of his boat, and carefully tucked the lacquered box under his arm. As he looked about, he noticed that the houses appeared oddly different, too. Old trees were gone. New ones twisted where none had been. Urashima began to run in the direction of his home. The temple was not where it was supposed to be. Faces he did not recognize filled the streets. He could hardly breathe in his confusion as he ran up and down the roads trying to find his way. At last he stopped an old man on the road and asked about his family's house.

"Those people lived in this village a long time ago," replied the old man. "Their son Urashima the fisherman rowed out to sea one day and never returned. They died of broken hearts."

"I am their son!" Urashima cried miserably. "How wicked I have been to stay away so long!"

The old man squinted at Urashima and said, "This happened three hundred years ago! You must be dreaming. Urashima is dead. Look and see for yourself in the graveyard."

Urashima clutched the lacquered box to his chest and ran to the graveyard. He searched the gravestones. He saw his mother's name, his father's name, and then ... his own name.

"How can this be?" Urashima screamed in despair, and ran back to the beach.

Wild with grief and confusion, he sat on the sand beside his boat. He held the box and rocked and moaned, "How can this be?"

As tears streamed down his face, Urashima stared at the lacquered box. An overwhelming desire to open it filled him. "Perhaps the answer to this mystery is inside," he thought. He tore apart the silver rope and opened the box. For a fleeting moment he saw the disappointed face of his beloved float before him. As quickly as it had appeared, it vanished.

A timeless, foul smelling vapor drifted out of the box and surrounded Urashima's body. Within moments, his face began to wrinkle. His hands clawed with age. His back became bent and gnarled. The hair on his head turned snow white and then fell to the ground. His vision blurred and his teeth fell out. His body, crushed under the weight of three hundred years of aging, shriveled and shrank until Urashima was a pile of dust blown bit by bit out to sea.

Mother Holle

A FOLKTALE FROM GERMANY

There was once a tired old widow who had two daughters. One was kind and hard-working. The other was mean and lazy. The kind daughter helped her mother do all the hard work of the household. The mean daughter was rude and unpleasant about her chores. It wasn't worth the widow's heartache to make her do much of anything. No amount of scolding could budge her from her lazy ways.

One day, the hard-working daughter was spinning wool beside the well when she pricked her finger on the spindle. A drop of blood stained the wood. She leaned over into the well to wash it off, and the spindle slipped from her fingers and tumbled into the water.

"Oh no!" she cried, "I must get my spindle back!" She jumped in after it.

The water bubbled and swirled about her head as she sank into the depths of the dark well. She fell deeper and deeper through the water until she landed softly in the middle of a bright grassy meadow.

Startled at where she'd landed, she stood up, straightened her skirts, smoothed her hair, and looked around. A pitiful moaning and weeping were coming from an oven at the edge of the meadow.

"Help me! I'm burning! Open the door and take me out!" said the voice.

Walking toward the sound, she opened the oven and saw that it was a loaf of bread complaining of the heat.

"I'll help you," she said, reaching far into the blazing oven. She pulled out the loaf, set it down and continued on her way.

Not far along she came upon an apple tree whose large branches were so

full of fruit they arched downward and touched the ground. "Please help me," said the tree. "Pick some of my apples and lighten my burden."

"Certainly, I'll help you," she said. The girl picked red apples until the tree's branches stretched upwards again. The tree swayed goodbye in the breeze as she continued on her way.

Soon she came to a brook gagged by a clump of leaves. "Please clear these leaves away," said the brook. "They are choking me!"

"I can clear the leaves for you," she said. The girl reached into the mud and removed the leaves until the brook ran swiftly on its way.

The girl went on until she came to a cottage in the woods. At the doorway stood a gnarled old woman with huge white teeth. The woman smiled broadly as she asked, "Will you help me shake these feather pillows and make the snow blow all over the mountains?"

"Yes I will, old woman," said the girl. She shook the pillows with such energy, the old woman was pleased and said, "I am Mother Holle. If you stay with me and sweep my floor, I will feed you well and you will gain what you deserve."

The girl was tired and hungry by this time, but she did as Mother Holle asked. After she swept every piece of dust out of the house, she ate a fine meal and fell into a blissful sleep near the fire.

The kindhearted girl stayed with Mother Holle for a long time. She swept the floor spotless and shook the feather pillows with joy. But happy as she was, the girl soon became homesick and said to Mother Holle, "I want to see my own mother again."

Mother Holle replied, "You may leave whenever you like. For your hard work you will receive what you deserve. Here is your lost spindle. Walk through my back door and see what you will see."

The girl walked through the back door and found herself in the grassy meadow again. A gentle rain began to fall as she walked along. The raindrops turned into shining golden coins that clung to her dress. The golden raindrops dripped around her fingers until each hand had five beautiful rings. Before she knew it, she was in front of her own house. The rooster on the gate crowed in welcome,

"Cocka doodle do! Cocka doodle do!
The kindhearted girl's come home to you!
Golden rings on her fingers,
golden coins on her clothes,
she smiles and shines,
wherever she goes!"

Her mother and sister rushed out to greet her. "Where did you get all this gold?" her mother asked. The girl told the tale of how she had jumped into the well after the bloody spindle and met Mother Holle.

"She gave me these coins for shaking her feather pillows and sweeping her floor."

The mean-hearted sister was so jealous of this good fortune she decided to go and get some gold all for herself. "How hard could it be to shake and sweep?" she thought.

She grabbed the spindle, poked the cat to get a drop of blood, and ran to the well. She threw down the spindle and jumped right in after it. She landed in the middle of the same grassy meadow.

A voice cried at the edge of the meadow, "Help me! I'm burning! Open the door and take me out!"

Walking toward the sound, she saw that it was a loaf of bread complaining of the heat.

"I'll not help you," she said, wrinkling her face into a pruny frown. "I might burn my fingers. If I opened the oven door, the heat would make me sweat uncomfortably. You've gotten yourself into your own trouble. It's no concern of mine." And she continued on her way.

Not far along, she came upon the apple tree whose large branches were so full of fruit they arched downward and touched the ground. "Please help me," said the tree. "Pick some of my apples and lighten my burden."

"Why should I take the time to pick your apples?" said the grumpy girl, tossing her head back and tapping her foot impatiently. "Besides, some hard apples might fall on me with a bump! I'll just take one to eat," she said, roughly ripping an apple from a low branch. She munched it and continued on.

Soon she came to the brook gagged by a clump of leaves. "Please clear these leaves away," said the brook. "They are choking me!"

The girl snickered and said, "Stupid brook! I am not so crazy as to put my delicate hands into your mucky mud." She turned up her nose and walked on.

At last she came to the cottage in the woods. At the doorway stood the gnarled old woman with huge white teeth. "Will you help me shake these feather pillows and make the snow blow all over the mountains?" the old woman asked.

Now the girl knew all about Mother Holle from what her sister had said. She pretended to be willing to work and shook the pillows for all she was worth.

"I am Mother Holle," said the old woman. "If you stay with me and sweep my floor, I will feed you well and you will gain what you deserve."

The girl was anxious for gold and agreed to sweep the floor. She swept as best as she could, never having swept before. Quickly weary from her effort, she ate a large meal and slept soundly by the fire.

The next day the girl shook the pillow only once. When a feather or two flew, she announced that she was done. Then she swiped at the floor with a quick swish and was finished. Each day she ate her fill and did less and less work. Finally she said, with a snip and a sigh, "Old hag, you've made me work my poor hands to the bone. I want to go home with my spindle and my reward."

Mother Holle replied, "You may leave whenever you like. As for your hard work, you will receive what you deserve. Here is your lost spindle and some catnip for the cat. Walk through my back door and see what you will see."

The girl walked through the back door and found herself in the grassy meadow again. As she walked along, a gentle rain began to fall. The raindrops turned into sticky black tar and clung to her dress and hair. The raindrops dripped around her fingers until each hand was gloved in pitch. She fumed and raged. Sticky and miserable, she ranted and ran until she was in front of her own house. The cat screeched. The rooster on the gate crowed,

"Cocka doodle do! Cocka doodle do!
The mean-hearted girl's come home to you!
Sticky tar on her fingers,
sticky tar on her clothes,
she's sour and sullen,
wherever she goes!"

The kindhearted girl and her mother tried to help wash the sticky tar away. They put the mean-hearted sister in a tub of warm water and soap. But she tartly cursed and grotesquely grumbled. They scrubbed and scrubbed until she almost dissolved in the suds.

It was no use.
She wouldn't mend her ways.
The sticky tar stuck tight,
'til the end of her days.

The Sealskin

A FOLKTALE FROM ICELAND

The sea pounded the rocky Icelandic shore and slid, like a foaming mirror, back into itself. A young Fisherman climbed the boulders along the water's edge. The brisk wind whipped his face. He made his way toward a cave opening, seeking shelter from the sea spray. As he approached, he heard sweet singing drifting out of the darkness. Coming closer, he saw black sealskins draped over the rocks at the edge of the cave. He crept silently toward one of the skins and snatched it away. Clutching it tightly, he hid behind a rock and stared at the cave opening.

Before long, beautiful, dark-eyed women emerged from the cave, dressed themselves in the sealskins, and returned to the sea. One woman, however, stayed behind, searching frantically everywhere. Finally, with a shiver and a sigh, she sat sadly on a rock and wept.

The Fisherman felt his heart swell with an unexplainable longing for the woman. His love for her swept his good sense away and he could think of nothing but bringing her home with him. He hid her sealskin under some stones and approached the strange woman. She did not flee. He put his coat over her bare shoulders. Speaking only with his eyes, he led her to his house.

He fed her fish cakes and warm broth. She fell asleep on his bed. The Fisherman listened to her quiet, even breathing. He admired her long black hair, spread like seaweed over his pillows. He wanted her to stay. When her sleep was deep, he dashed back to the shore, took the sealskin from its hiding place and brought it home with him. While the beautiful woman slept, he hid the skin inside a great chest and locked the lid. The key went into his pocket and he promised himself that he would carry it with him always.

Days, weeks, and then months passed. The Fisherman treated his unusual visitor so tenderly that she soon loved him and they were married. To the villagers, they seemed happy enough. But the woman never spoke, and some days she sat for hours on the rocks at the water's edge. Her dark eyes gazed sullenly at the swelling sea.

Time passed, and they had seven children together. She cared for them well. But every day the woman would take her children to the edge of the ocean. They would play in the sand as she looked out to sea. Her dark eyes always had such a faraway, sad look.

One Sunday, the Fisherman took all the children to town. His wife had felt ill and stayed at home. As soon as he was gone, she gathered his work clothes, scattered in the rush of leaving. A strange key fell from his shirt pocket and landed with a clatter on the floor.

It was a mysterious key to the woman, for she had never seen it before. She held it in her hand and looked about the cottage to see what it could open. The chest, covered with a cloth, was long used as a bench. She lifted the covering and pushed the key into the welcoming hole.

Hidden in the shadows of the chest she saw the black sealskin.

A gasp washed over her like a wave. She remembered the taste of the ocean and the surging of the tides. She reached into the darkness and pried the sealskin from its hiding place. She grasped it to her heart and dashed out of the door, running, tripping, stumbling to the sea. Slipping the skin on, she slid into the water. An eerie song floated over the waves. Some say they heard it.

> *"I've seven children on the land,*
> *and seven in the sea.*
> *My heart is torn,*
> *for those I've born.*
> *Salt tears, my choice must be."*

She never returned. Yet, whenever the Fisherman's children walked along the beach, a black seal swam close to shore, tossing jellyfish and colorful shells up on the land to delight them. The Fisherman's nets were always full of codfish. He said that there was a dark-eyed seal who swam about his boat, splashing the good catch his way.

The Tiger, the Brahman, and the Jackal

A FOLKTALE FROM INDIA

One hot day in ancient India, a poor Brahman kicked up dust as he walked along the road with his begging bowl in hand. He heard a roar and a rattling coming from around the bend. A fierce tiger paced and growled inside a bamboo cage. The huge beast anxiously pawed the bars and shook the hinges.

The Brahman was a kind man who could not bear to see suffering. As he approached the cage, the tiger pleaded, "Set me free! If I stay in this cage I am doomed."

The Brahman timidly replied, "Just promise that you will not eat me once I set you free."

"Of course I will not eat you," purred the tiger. "I would be grateful to you for your goodness and mercy."

The Brahman opened the bamboo cage and the tiger sprang out to freedom. The huge cat whirled around, and whipped his long tail side to side. "I am hungry," he snarled. "I was in that trap for such a long time. I will eat you."

"Wait!" cried the trembling man. "It is not fair for you to eat me after I have saved your life."

"Fair?" laughed the tiger wickedly. "It is my nature. I am hungry and you are food. It is proper that I should eat you."

"It is never proper to repay kindness with cruelty," stated the Brahman.

"You are only thinking of yourself," said the hungry tiger. "Yet I will show you how reasonable I can be. I will not eat you if three things agree that it is unfair."

45

"Very well," said the Brahman, "I will go and ask the next three things I meet about this matter. I promise to return shortly with their opinions."

"Come back quickly," warned the tiger.

The Brahman turned and walked down the road. The first thing he came upon was a tree. "Oh, tree," he said, "do you think that it is fair to repay kindness with cruelty?"

The tree rustled its leaves and replied, "I give shade. I give my fruit. When I am old or if I become rotten, people will cut me down. They will chop me up for firewood. You are a fool to expect kindness in return for your kindness."

"Thank you for your opinion," said the Brahman. He continued down the road.

The next thing he met was a buffalo yoked to the wheel of a well. Slowly the animal struggled to turn the wheel.

"Pardon me, old buffalo," said the Brahman. "I need your opinion about a matter that is quite important to me. Do you think it is fair to repay kindness with cruelty?"

The buffalo strained at her load. She slowly replied, "When I was young, I generously gave people abundant, rich milk. They fed me the finest cottonseed and oil cake. Now that I am old and dry, my food is garbage. I am forced to work until I drop with exhaustion each night. This is how my kindness has been rewarded. Do not ask me if it is fair. It is the way things are, unfortunately."

"Thank you for your opinion," said the Brahman, who sadly continued on his way.

"I am doomed," he thought as he went along. He looked down and asked the road for its opinion.

The road replied, "I lead people wherever they wish to go. How is my goodness rewarded? I am trampled and rutted until I am a miserable mess. That is the way things are."

"I see," said the Brahman, who sighed and started back down the road toward the hungry tiger.

An old jackal, sitting in the sun beside the road, noticed the Brahman walking by and said,

"Good day, dear sir!
You look so sad to me.
I pity your miserable mood.
What could the matter be?"

"I am unhappy," moaned the Brahman, "because I am doomed to death as a reward for my kindness. I freed a tiger from a cage and now he plans to eat me. I am traveling to him now so that I can be his meal."

The jackal cocked his head one way and then the other.

"You must take me to the cage.
I cannot picture what you say.
How could the tiger eat you
in this most ungrateful way?"

"Come with me," said the Brahman. "I will show you exactly how it happened."

The jackal and the Brahman arrived at the bend in the road where the tiger stretched and scratched himself lazily in the sun. When the tiger saw the Brahman approaching, he leaped to his feet and said, "It is about time! You have made me wait and I am hungry. Let us begin the meal immediately."

"Before the meal begins," said the Brahman, resigned to his fate, "give me a moment to explain this event to my friend, the jackal."

"Yes, please wait," said the jackal,

"I am confused about what happened …
It has been explained to me.
But I do not understand.
Can you try to help me see?"

"See what?" roared the tiger, impatiently drooling over the trembling Brahman.

The jackal replied,

"How did it come to pass
that you are going to eat this man?

*Explain it simply to me.
I'll try to understand."*

The tiger roared, "He simply set me free from this trap and now I am going to eat him! That is all. Now, let's get on with the meal."

The jackal shook his head and muttered. "I have it now …

*This man was in the trap
and you set him free?
Pardon my confusion,
but it makes no sense to me."*

"No! Fool!" shouted the tiger, "*I* was in the trap and he set *me* free. Now I am going to eat him."

The jackal thought out loud …

*"You and the man were in the trap.
He was seated on your lap …"*

"No!" roared the tiger, "*I* was in the trap when the man walked by!"

The jackal's eyes brightened. He clapped his paws and jumped about, shouting,

*"Yes! Yes! It's as clear as the sky …
You were in the man
when the trap walked by …"*

"NNNOOOO!" roared the tiger, "I was in the *trap!!!*"

The jackal shouted,

*"You were in the trap!
Oh, this makes my head spin …
You were in the trap …
But how did you get in?"*

"I will show you," roared the furious tiger. "Then go away and let me eat in peace or I will eat you, too!"

The tiger jumped into the trap, but before he could leap out, the jackal shut the cage door and locked it.

The Brahman watched with wide-eyed amazement.

"Let me out!" demanded the tiger.

But the jackal grinned and said,

> *"I finally understand today,*
> *where, tiger, you deserve to stay.*
> *Without another thought, dear sir,*
> *let us leave things as they were ..."*

With that, the jackal and the Brahman left the roaring tiger behind and continued down the hot dusty road.

Wiley and the Hairy Man

A FOLKTALE FROM THE UNITED STATES

"The Hairy Man is a wicked conjurer," warned Wiley's mother. "Be careful when you go out to chop firewood or he'll put you in his magic bag."

"Don't worry, Mamma," said Wiley, lifting his ax onto his shoulder, "I am smarter than any conjure man in these southern swamps."

"Then keep your wits about you," she said.

Wiley went out to the barn and tied his three hound dogs to the fence with a rope. Then he strode into the woods whistling and singing,

"I'm not afraid of the Hairy Man.
Come and get me if you can!"

Suddenly, Wiley heard footsteps behind him. He turned and saw a tall hulking figure covered all over with hair walking toward him, holding a sack. The figure's eyes gleamed red and his long sharp teeth poked through his drooling, twisted grin.

Wiley froze for a moment and gaped at the hooves he saw sticking out of the bottom of the figure's trousers. He dropped his ax and climbed a nearby bay tree as fast as his legs and arms would carry him. "I've never seen a cow climb a tree," he said to himself, as he clutched a branch. "I'll be safe up here."

The figure stopped in front of the tree and pulled open the sack with his hairy fingers. Wiley called down nervously, "What have you got in that sack?"

"Nothing yet …" chuckled the Hairy Man. "But soon enough I'll have you!" The Hairy Man lifted the ax that Wiley had dropped and began to chop

51

down the bay tree.

> *"Chop, Chop, I'll get you in my sack!*
> *Chop, Chop, I'll get you in my sack!"*

Now Wiley's mamma was a conjure woman and had taught him a trick or two. Wiley rubbed his belly against the trunk of the tree and sang over and over,

> *"Chip, Chip, fly on back!*
> *Chip, Chip, fly on back!"*

Each time Wiley sang, the chip of wood the Hairy Man chopped flew right back and stuck to the tree again!

The Hairy Man kept on chopping, *"Chop, Chop, I'll get you in my sack!"*

Wiley kept on singing. *"Chip, Chip, fly on back!"*

The woods echoed with *"Chop, Chop, I'll get you in my sack!"* *"Chip, Chip, fly on back!"* until Wiley and the Hairy Man were both exhausted. "Stop singing that!" screamed the Hairy Man.

"You are not so powerful," said Wiley craftily. "Why, I bet you couldn't turn yourself into a giraffe."

"I could so. Just watch!" said the Hairy Man, turning himself into a giraffe.

"Well, it is easy to turn yourself into something big," Wiley scoffed. "But I bet you couldn't turn yourself into something small … like an opossum."

"I could so. Just watch!" said the Hairy Man, turning himself into an opossum.

The moment the Hairy Man became an opossum, Wiley scampered down the tree and grabbed the magic bag that was lying on the ground. He quickly scooped up the opossum and put it in the bag. He tied the top and threw it into the river. Then he started running and laughing! *"I'm not afraid of the Hairy Man. Come and get me if you can!"*

Wiley stopped to catch his breath. Over his shoulder, he saw a huge, wet figure loping toward him, carrying a bag. It was the Hairy Man! Wiley tried to appear calm. "Hello, Hairy Man! How did you get out of the sack?"

"I turned myself into the wind and blew myself away," sneered the evil creature, reaching out to grab Wiley. Wiley leaped aside and said, "You are not as powerful as you think. I have a magic rope around my waist. I bet you can't make it disappear."

"I could make all the rope in the world disappear if I wanted to!" bragged the Hairy Man.

"Then I dare you to try!" Wiley taunted.

The Hairy Man puffed out his chest and cried,

"Rope! Rope! Listen here!
Rope! Rope! Disappear!"

The rope around Wiley's waist vanished and he had to grab his pants to hold them up. At the same moment, the rope that held his three hound dogs tied to the fence back home disappeared, too.

"Come here, dogs!" Wiley cried, knowing that the Hairy Man was afraid of dogs. When the Hairy Man heard the hound dogs come howling and barking, he turned and ran, as fast as he could, back into the swamp. Wiley kicked his heels and scampered on home.

"Mamma!" he yelled as he ran toward the house. "Open the door! The Hairy Man has been trying to get me in his sack!" He dashed inside and breathlessly told his Mamma what had happened so far.

"Well," Mamma considered, "You've outwitted him once and fooled him twice. If he's fooled one more time, he will have no more power over us. Now let me think about this."

Mamma sat in her rocking chair by the fireplace, rocked and thought a bit. Wiley locked all the windows and doors and made a big fire in the fireplace so the Hairy Man couldn't come down the chimney.

"Quick!" Mamma said, suddenly getting an idea. "Go fetch me the new little piglet that's sucking on the sow in the barn."

When Wiley returned with the little pig, Mamma tied a neat bonnet around its head and tucked it into Wiley's bed. Just then there was a pounding at the door.

Wiley peeked through a knothole, "It's the Hairy Man!" he said.

Mamma didn't open the door but she hollered loudly,

> *"Hairy Man, Hairy Man, standing at the door,*
> *if I give you my young one,*
> *will you go away*
> *and bother us no more?"*

Wiley couldn't believe his ears! He dashed up into the attic to hide.
A booming voice from the other side of the door answered,

> *"I'm the Hairy Man. I'm the Hairy Man, standing at your door.*
> *If you give me your young one,*
> *I'll go away*
> *and bother you no more."*

"Well then, come in and take my young one," said Mamma. "He's right here in the bed."

The door crashed open and the Hairy Man came in looking for the bed. He found it and ripped off the covers. "Wait!" he cried, "this is not your young one, it's a pig!"

"I promised you my young one, Hairy Man. I just didn't say which young one. This is my youngest piglet, and he was mine before I gave him to you. A promise between conjurers is a promise. Now do as you said, go away and bother us no more."

The Hairy Man knew he'd been outsmarted but there was nothing he could do about it. He raged as he grabbed the piglet from the bed, "I can't defeat a conjure woman who knows how to use her head!"

Out the door he stormed, with the piglet under his arm. He tore up trees everywhere he went. The next morning folks said that a cyclone must have come through in the night. Wiley and his Mamma chuckled because they knew *that* wasn't true.

The Golden Goose

A FOLKTALE FROM GERMANY

*O*nce there were three brothers who lived with their parents in the green woods. The two older sons were rough, hearty fellows. The younger brother was gentle and kind. He freed the birds his brothers caught in their snares, and they called him Simpleton.

One day the oldest son prepared to go into the forest to cut firewood. His father gave him a sharp ax and a pat on the back. His mother gave him honey cake and sweet wine to drink. He walked with long powerful strides into the woods.

Deep in the forest, he passed a little gray-haired man sitting by the side of the path. "Please," said the man, "give me a bit of your cake and a sip of your wine. My tongue is parched and my belly is empty."

"I am no fool!" said the son. "If I give you some food, I will have less for myself."

The young man walked away to chop a large oak. As soon as he swung his ax, he cut his arm, and had to go home to be mended.

The second son set out for the forest carrying a huge ax over his shoulder. He had honey cake and a flask of wine in his sack. Beside the path, he met the gray-haired man, who pleaded, "Be kind and share your meal."

"No," said the second son. "If I give you some food, then there will be less for me." And he walked straight away into the woods to chop down a maple tree. As soon as he swung his ax, he cut his leg and had to go hobbling home.

"Then I will go and cut firewood," said Simpleton. "Parents, please give me food and an ax just as you have given my injured brothers."

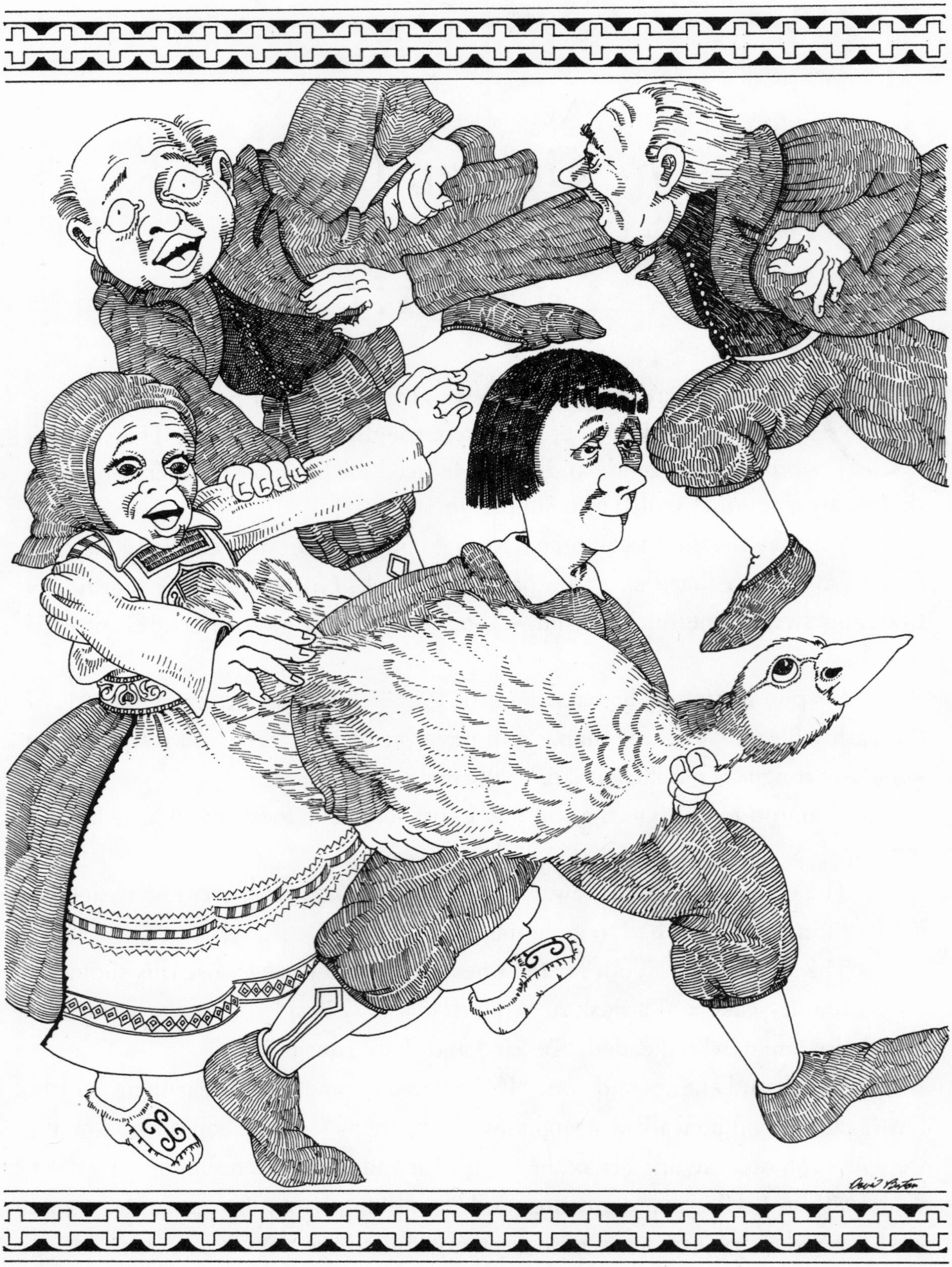

But his mother fretted and said, "Your two strong brothers were hurt today in the woods. Stay home where it is safe."

His father scoffed, "If I gave you an ax you would pity the tree and not cut a branch."

But he begged so long that his father gave him a small dull hatchet, and his mother gave him bread baked in the ashes, and a bottle of water. Off he went whistling into the woods.

Before long he came upon the little gray-haired man who said, "I am hungry. Would you share your food with me?"

"Well, surely I would," said Simpleton, "but it is only ash bread and water. I'm happy to give the best that I have, although it's not very much at all."

"Nonsense," said the gray-haired man with a smile, "it is quite remarkable to share the best that you have."

They sat together to eat. When the boy opened his sack he discovered, to his amazement, sweet raisin cakes. Wine flowed from his flask! They ate and drank their fill. "Take my advice," said the old man, "and go to the fallen tree at the edge of the forest. Split open the trunk and see what is there for you as a reward for your kindness."

Simpleton rushed to the edge of the forest and split the tree trunk with his hatchet. The trunk opened like a large brown hand and there, sitting in its roots, was a squawking goose with golden feathers. He lifted the golden goose under his arm and set off down the road.

As night darkened the forest, he came to an inn. He entered and called for a table. With the goose beside him, he feasted on a tasty meal. The goose honked and ate barley seeds from a silver dish. When it came time to pay the bill, Simpleton plucked a feather from the bird's tail and handed it to the innkeeper's daughter. Her eyes stared wide as she fingered the golden feather in her hand. She offered Simpleton the inn's best room for the night.

At midnight, as Simpleton slept with the golden goose beside him, the innkeeper's daughter and her two younger sisters crept along the hallway to Simpleton's room. The oldest daughter hushed her sisters and tiptoed across the bedroom floor to snatch another golden feather or two. The moment she touched the bird's tail, which was poking out from under the covers, she stuck fast to it. Her sisters peeked in the doorway and saw their older sister struggling to get away. Rushing to pull her free, one grabbed her arm and one grabbed her waist. Their hands stuck fast the moment they touched her. They pulled and pulled, but there was no help for it. The three stuck to the goose for the rest of the night, while both boy and bird slept pleasantly.

In the morning, Simpleton gathered up the golden goose under his arm. Without a word to the three girls stuck to the bird's tail, he headed out the door and went whistling down the road.

As the three girls stumbled along behind Simpleton, the church Parson saw the trio and scolded them. "Stop chasing after that boy! It is not proper or polite!" He grabbed hold of the youngest sister's skirt and tried to pull her off the parade. The moment the Parson touched the skirt, he stuck fast and was dragged along. Simpleton kept walking and did not look back once.

They went past the church Sexton who cried out, "Parson, let go of that young girl's skirt! It is a disgrace to see you chasing her so." The Sexton grabbed hold of the Parson's coattails and stuck fast too.

This zany parade passed in front of the King's palace. There, the Princess sat on her balcony, serious and sullen. She had never laughed in all her life. The King fretted so much about her sorrow, he offered half his kingdom and his daughter's hand in marriage to the first young man who could make her smile. When the Princess glanced out and saw the strange parade led by the whistling boy and his golden goose, a grin cracked her stony expression. She laughed out loud.

When the King heard her laugh for the first time, it was as though a thousand bells had rung. "Who has caused this miracle?" he cried, and rushed out to see.

"Oh no!" cried the King, "It is a peasant boy with a goose! He is not fit to marry a Princess!"

But the girl was delighted with the boy and commanded the servants to bring Simpleton immediately before the throne. The moment Simpleton set the golden goose down, his odd companions tumbled to the floor, and the Princess laughed so hard her sides ached. The Parson and the Sexton bowed, the innkeeper's three blushing daughters curtsied, and they all fled.

The Princess smiled at Simpleton and Simpleton smiled shyly back. This attraction alarmed the King. He blustered, "In spite of the fact that you have made her smile, you may not have my daughter's hand in marriage unless you bring me a man who can drink my wine cellar dry." Thinking this to be an impossible task, the King sent Simpleton away.

The boy returned to the forest and found the gray-haired man sitting alongside the road smacking his parched lips. "Oh, what a thirst I have," he complained, "I could drink a lake."

"How strange that you should be so thirsty!" said Simpleton. "The King asked me to find a man who can drink his wine cellar dry."

In as short a time as it takes to tell it, the gray-haired man went to the palace and drank every drop in all the barrels of the King's wine cellar.

"Well," sputtered the King, seeing this remarkable thirst, "in spite of what I have said before, you cannot marry my daughter until you bring me a man who can eat a mountain of bread."

The gray-haired man wiped the wine from his chin. He said with a grin, "Bake it and I will eat it for this lad's happiness."

The royal bakers piled a mountain of loaves in the middle of the town square. The gray-haired man ate the mountain to the last crumb, patted his belly, and returned to the forest.

The Princess was pleased when Simpleton returned to the throne room to say, "The mountain of bread is gone! I will ask for my bride's hand now."

But the King came between them and said, "No! I forbid you to marry my daughter until you bring me a ship that sails on land or water."

Simpleton sadly left the palace for the woods and headed home with his goose under his arm. He came upon the gray-haired man, who asked, "Why do you look so unhappy?"

Simpleton sighed and replied, "The King has commanded me to bring him a ship that sails on land or sea. Surely such a boat is impossible to find."

The old man said, "It is not as rare as kindness! I will help you again for sharing your food with me when I was hungry in the woods."

Before Simpleton could blink, the gray-haired man turned into a remarkable gray ship that floated above the ground. Huge sails billowed in the wind as Simpleton climbed aboard. The ship floated up over the trees with the golden goose at the helm. It landed in the King's courtyard. The Princess's cheeks ached from grinning as the boy stepped down the plank. "Be my bride," he said with a deep bow.

The King saw the happy face on his daughter and finally said, "Anyone who can make a woman smile this often will be a fine husband indeed. If you truly wish this match, dear daughter, you have my blessings."

The Princess agreed to the wedding and the Parson married them then and there. As crowds cheered, Simpleton and the Princess climbed aboard the magic ship and set sail for adventure in faraway lands.

The Magic Oysters
of the Queen of the South Sea

A FOLKTALE FROM INDONESIA

Great flood waves rushed across the river. Winds howled as buffaloes, crops, and people were swept away during a southwest monsoon. When the storm subsided, Pak Sidin and his wife gathered what was left of their family and belongings. They sadly looked at the muddy wasteland that had been their fine rice field. Now, instead of living in a sturdy house of closely woven bamboo and palm leaves, they crouched for shelter in a tumbledown hut beside the river.

"What will we do?" wept Pak Sidin's wife, Munah. "We have only two *batoks** of rice and one of grain," she said, measuring their food in half coconut shell bowls.

Pak Sidin was hopeful. "I spoke today with the men who earn their living by collecting bird nests high in the cliff caves beside the sea. I could join them."

"It is a fine idea," said Munah, "but what of your fear of Ratu Loro Kidul?"† Munah knew how much her husband dreaded the Queen of the South Sea.

"Her raging waves and swift tides bring terror to my heart," he said, trembling as he spoke. "But we have no money to buy buffaloes or rice plants. I cannot be a farmer now. I must try to earn what I can. Tomorrow we will make an offering to the Sea Queen and ask for my safety as I climb down the cliffs."

"I will pray for you, dear husband," said Munah. "What do you wish to offer to Ratu Loro Kidul?"

---

* half of a coconut shell (bah-tok)
† the Queen of the South Sea (rah-too loh-roh kih-dool)

"Let us give the best we have," he said. "We will offer two *batoks* of rice. Color them red and yellow so that they are beautiful to see. I will carry them to the offering place in my finest cloth. Divide the grain between yourself and the children. I will fast."

"I hope you succeed," Munah said. "There is not much grain and our children are crying with hunger."

"We will offer the best we have to appease the Queen of the South Sea. I will work as hard as I can to find nests," he said. "What more can I do?"

In the morning Pak Sidin traveled with the other men to the cliffs. He walked beside Pak Moor, a rich cliff climber. Pak Moor's wife had prepared a sumptuous offering for Ratu Loro Kidul. He carried a roast chicken, fried fish, cooked rice, and bananas. Every few steps, Pak Moor reached into his pot and took a bite for himself. First he ate a chicken wing, and then a leg, some fish, and some rice. By the time they arrived at the edge of the cliffs, Pak Moor had only chicken bones and banana skins to place on the offering mat for Ratu Loro Kidul.

Unlike Pak Moor, Pak Sidin had not eaten even one grain of rice as he went along. Dizzy with hunger, Pak Sidin placed his offering on the mat and went toward the edge of the steep cliffs rising from the spray of pounding surf.

"Don't look down, Pak Sidin," the more experienced men warned, as they descended the cliff on hanging ladders. Pak Sidin swallowed hard and grasped his ladder so tightly his knuckles bulged. Slowly, he climbed down toward the sea. The ladders led to ropes. The men took hold of the ropes to swing themselves into caves along the cliff's face.

"Go into a cave that is close by," said one man. "Perhaps you will have some luck." Pak Sidin swung himself into the mouth of a nearby cave. He eyed the wall and floor of the damp salty place but saw no nests. Lying on a flat rock before him were large oysters.

"I shall bring some home for Munah to eat," he said to himself. "She has probably given all the grain to the children and kept none for herself."

"You may take the oysters!" said a swirling voice, which flowed around his head like the tide.

Pak Sidin whirled about to see who spoke. No one was there.

"Take them as a gift from me for your generous offering," said the voice, loud as a crashing wave. "Do not let anyone see them. They are just for you and your family."

Pak Sidin knew this invisible voice must be the Queen of the South Sea. He trembled and gathered the oysters into his headband and belt. He fled from the cave and grabbed the rope that swung him to the ladder. Drenched with ocean spray, he climbed up the cliff wall. His heart pounded like the waves crashing on the rocks below him.

Meanwhile, Pak Sidin's wife, Munah, sat waiting in the tumbledown hut, overwhelmed with worry. Unable to remain still any longer, she went to the ocean's edge. "Great and mighty Queen of the Sea," she cried out, "send my husband home to me safely!"

Pak Moor's wife also went to the edge of the water. She cried out, "Great and mighty Queen of the Sea! Please give us a fortune as great as my husband's offering was great!"

Pak Moor was still in a cave close to the surf. Drowsy from the huge meal of roast chicken, fish, and rice he had just eaten, he lay down and fell asleep on the cave floor. He slept so soundly he did not notice that the sky was darkening. He did not hear the fury of the swelling storm. A cold tidal wave crashed into the mouth of the cave. Pak Moor struggled against the surging water to stand up and reach the ropes. Lightning lit the cave with an eerie blue glow. A thunderous voice surrounded him, pounding him with sound. "Glutton! Why did you leave chewed bones as your offering? You deserve no pity from the Queen of the South Sea!"

Pak Moor splashed and stretched to reach the rope at the cave's mouth, only to be smashed back against the cave walls with each wave. "I was hungry!" he said. "Pity me for the sake of my wife and children!"

The Queen of the South Sea roared, "I have heard the words of your wife. She is crying out to me, at this moment. I will give her what she asks. Go home now, or I will drag you to the depths of the ocean where the octopuses will squeeze your life's breath away!"

The rope floated to Pak Moor on the arm of a wave. He sputtered and grabbed it, pulling himself half-drowned out of the cave and toward the ladders. As he climbed, the winds battered him. He thought, "I wonder what my wife requested? Surely she must have asked the Queen of the Sea for good fortune. That is always her wish!"

Pak Moor reached the cliff top and stumbled toward home. As he approached his house, his children and his wife came running toward him crying, "Lightning hit our house during the storm. It has burned to the ground!"

Pak Moor said, "I do not understand this misfortune! The Queen of the Sea told me that she would give you what you asked for. Wife, did you wish disaster upon us?"

"No!" his wife wept bitterly. "I wished for a fortune as great as the offering you gave."

Pak Moor's cheeks flushed with humiliation at his own greed. "I have brought this misfortune upon myself," he moaned. The charred skeleton of the house that stood before him looked as bare as the chewed bones he'd left for the Queen of the Sea.

Meanwhile, Pak Sidin rushed home to the tumbledown hut where his wife and children awaited him. He took off his belt and headband. The oysters he had gathered fell to the ground. "I found no nests, but at least you can eat these oysters," he said, opening them. To his amazement, inside each oyster was a large, round, lustrous pearl.

Pak Sidin sold the pearls at the market and was able to buy land, buffaloes, and rice plants again. He soon became a farmer, as rich in wealth as he was in generosity.

The Sad Story of Stone Frogs

AN ABORIGINAL FOLKTALE FROM AUSTRALIA

*A*s four young sisters scampered over mounds of large rocks hunting for mice and juicy lizards to eat, they came upon an old hunchbacked man. "You have an ugly bump on your back!" they teased.

The old man ignored their insult.

They continued annoying him. "You are as bumpy as the emu!" they taunted. "That silly, big brown bird cannot fly!"

The hunchback's voice exploded with rage, "Do not speak such words about my sacred *mah!** The emu is my tribe's totem animal!"

The hunchback was a *wirinun,†* a sorcerer. In a fury, he changed the girls into frogs, and left them hopping and croaking alongside the muddy pond.

Meanwhile, their mother searched for them frantically. A hard rain had fallen since the girls left their camp. Now the only footprints the mother saw were made by raindrops pitting the mud. She headed far from camp in her search, calling out for her daughters. At last she heard voices that she recognized. The voices seemed small and far away.

She followed the sounds to the edge of a muddy pond. At her feet she saw four fat frogs. She licked her lips and said, "I have traveled far and I am hungry. Oh, what a fine meal I shall have!" She caught two fat frogs in each fist. As they wriggled, she heard her daughters' voices.

"A powerful *wirinun* has changed us into frogs! Do not eat us! We are your children!"

---

* totem plant or animal sacred to clan
† medicine man, sorcerer (pronounced wirreenun)

67

The mother thought she must be dreaming. She brought the frogs toward her mouth and once again, she heard, "No! No! Don't eat us. We are your children!"

She looked deeply into the dark eyes of the frogs as they wriggled in front of her face. Horrified, she dropped them into the mud and ran to the dwelling of the sorcerer.

The *wirinun* was making a fire and did not look up when the woman ran breathlessly toward him.

"Did you change my daughters into frogs?" she gasped.

The *wirinun* was pleased that she could see how powerful he was. "Yes, I turned them into frogs. They insulted my *mah*. It is wrong to ridicule a sacred totem. The emu is my tribe's animal. My tribe should war with your tribe for this cruel insult. Instead I only turned your daughters into frogs. They earned their punishment with their mean words."

"Please," she begged, "take back your magic and make them into girls again."

"They cannot take back their words. I cannot take back my magic," he said simply.

"But you are powerful!" she pleaded. "You must try and change them back. Someone will eat them!"

"Then you should eat them," said the sorcerer. "Why waste good food?"

"How can you speak like this!" the woman wailed. "I cannot eat my children." Then she said in desperation, "I do not want anyone to eat them … I will trade you myself for your magic. I will come and live in your house as your wife."

"When I was young," said the *wirinun* spitefully, "you scorned me because of my humpback. I do not want you now that you are old. Let the husband you chose instead of me change them back!" He ignored her and began to carve a picture on a boomerang with an opossum's tooth.

The old woman winced, remembering how she had ridiculed his humpback when she was young. Seeing that he would not take her, she offered her most precious possession. "I will give you my *doori*.* This magical grinding stone belonged to my father's father's father! It grunts when anyone but its rightful owner touches it! I will make it yours."

"That is interesting to me," said the old man.

The woman ran to her dwelling and came back with the *doori*. She gave her dearest possession to the *wirinun*.

He fingered it and smiled wryly. "Yes, for this stone I will change your daughters. I promise that now no one can ever eat them."

The woman sighed a great sigh, and ran off into the bush to find her daughters.

She looked for them frantically all around the pond where she had left them. She did not see them. She did not hear them. Then she looked down at the edge of the water. She saw the frogs and began to wail and shake as if she was mourning.

"Oh wicked *wirinun*! Yes, my daughters will never be eaten!" she said bitterly as she reached down to pick up the silent frogs. Some were gray and some had a stripe of green. She clutched them to her chest and wept, for they were all turned to stone.

---

* a grinding stone

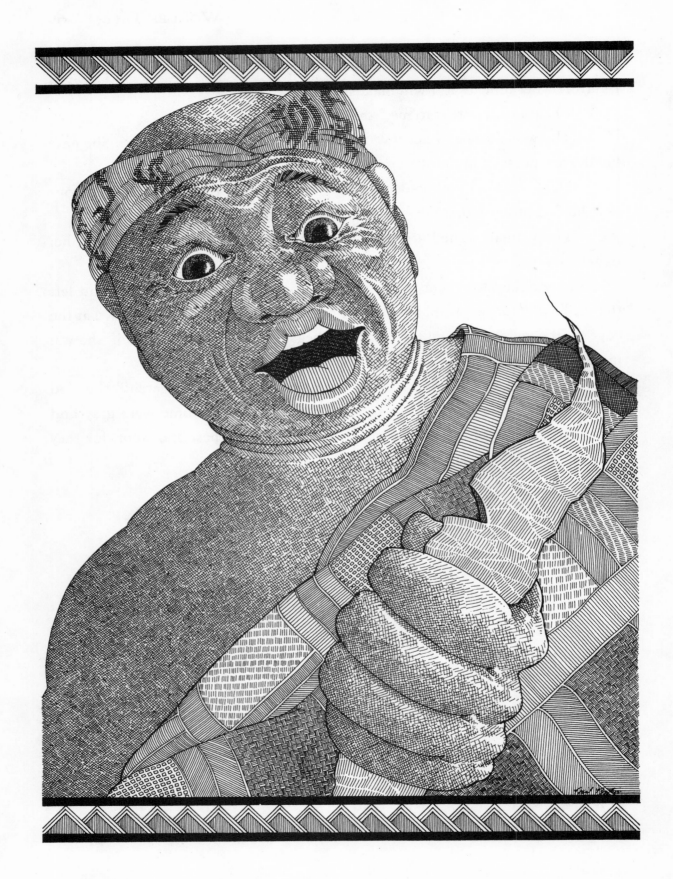

Talk! Talk!

An Ashanti Folktale from West Africa

Talk! Talk!
Can you believe that talk?
Talk! Talk!
Can you believe that talk?

I don't know
if it's true.
It was told to me,
so I tell it to you!

 farmer was digging yams one day. Suddenly one of his yams said, "Ouch! You are hurting me!" Whoa! The man jumped back and ran down the road.

Talk! Talk!
Can you believe that talk?
Talk! Talk!
Can you believe that talk?

He came upon a fisherman and said, "My yam talked to me!"

"That's ridiculous," said the fisherman, pulling up his net. "Yams can't talk."

"I certainly agree!" said the net.

Whoa! The farmer and the fisherman ran down the road.

Talk! Talk!
Can you believe that talk?
Talk! Talk!
Can you believe that talk?

They came upon a man swimming in the river, and shouted together, "Strange things are happening!"

The farmer exclaimed, "My yam talked to me."

The fisherman said, "My fishing net spoke!"

"That's ridiculous!" said the swimmer. "Yams can't speak and fishing nets don't talk!"

"That's absolutely true," said the river.

Whoa! The farmer, the fisherman and the swimmer ran down the road to tell the King.

Talk! Talk!
Can you believe that talk?
Talk! Talk!
Can you believe that talk?

They rushed into the King's hut and shouted together, "Strange things are happening!"

The farmer exclaimed, "My yam talked to me."

The fisherman cried, "My fishing net spoke!"

The swimmer sputtered, "The river talked too!"

The King scowled and raged and said, "Go home, foolish people! Stop spreading ridiculous rumors!"

The farmer, the fisherman, and the swimmer left the hut.

The King sat on his royal stool and muttered to himself, "When people tell ridiculous, untrue stories, it alarms the community ... everywhere ...."

"You are absolutely right ..." said his chair!

Talk! Talk!
Can you believe that talk?
Talk! Talk!
Can you believe that talk?

I don't know
if it's true.
It was told to me,
so I tell it to you!

The Man Who Could Transform Himself

A FOLKTALE FROM KENYA

There were once two brothers who were very poor. They were orphans and had nothing in the world to sustain them but two cows. One day the older brother took both cows to a magician and said, "I will trade you these two cows if you can give me some magical powers."

"One must know how to use the powers wisely," said the magician, eyeing the cattle.

"I will be careful and use the powers to help others," said the older brother.

"Very well then, I will teach you how to transform yourself into any animal you want to be," said the magician, taking the two cows as payment.

When the brother had received a charm to change himself, he ran home as fast as his legs would carry him. He became tired as he ran and, transforming himself into a bird, he soared home. He landed on the ground in front of his younger brother and changed himself back into a man.

The younger brother gasped in amazement at what his brother could now do, but then he noticed that his brother had returned without their cows. He cried, "What use is this magic to us? We have no way to eat! At least before we could milk the cows!"

"Fear not, young brother," said the older one confidently. "You will soon see how I will use my powers to our benefit. Tomorrow when you look out of the window of our house you will see a great bull. It will be me! Take me to market and sell me for two cows and five goats. Do not disobey me! Do not tell anyone about my powers."

"I will do as you say," said the younger brother, curious to see the plan his brother had in mind.

The next morning, when the younger brother looked out of his window, there was a huge bull standing in the field. He walked to the bull and tied a rope around his neck. As he led the beast off to the marketplace, everyone exclaimed at his size. A rich man bought the bull for two cows and five goats. He planned to give the bull as a wedding gift to his bride's family. Delighted with the sale, the younger brother drove the cows and goats he had been paid to his own home.

The rich man tried to lead the bull down the road, but the animal charged him, knocked him down, and ran away. The bull galloped and bellowed. He snorted and ran. Clouds of dust rose at his hooves. The man chased after and bellowed just as loudly, "Come back! Come back!"

When the bull was out of sight, he turned the front half of himself into a lion. The footprints on the road were a confusion of bull and lion. Then he turned himself back into a man and sat calmly down beside the road. The rich man came huffing and puffing. "Have you seen a bull run by?" he asked the older brother.

"Yes," said the older brother, "a lion chased him. Look at the tracks!"

"Woe is me!" cried the rich man. "See how the lion has already eaten my bull. There was a great struggle! Now I've lost my bride's gift!"

The rich man turned sadly for home as the older brother jogged off, delighted with his greedy trick.

The next day the older brother wanted more goats and cows and said to his younger brother, "Let us do our market trading again. I will become a bull again. This time, trade me for three cows and eight goats. Soon we will be rich!"

In a blink, a huge bull was before the younger brother, who by now stood in awe of his older brother's power. He led the bull to market and immediately received the price he asked from a tall man who was delighted with the fine animal. "Come now," he said to the bull, "soon you will be a great feast."

The tall man drove the bull down the road to where he planned to slaughter him. But the bull began to run as before. He galloped and bellowed. He snorted and ran 'til the dust was a cloud at his hooves. The tall man ran after him shouting, "Come back! Come back!"

The bull stopped and faced the tall man. With a great snort, he turned himself into a lion and began to roar, thinking that this would frighten the tall man away.

But unknown to the older brother, the tall man who had purchased him was the magician in disguise. The tall man immediately turned himself into a lion too. He roared and charged.

The bull who had become a lion quickly turned himself into a bird. He flew upwards until his wings brushed the sky. The magician turned himself into a hawk and pursued the bird. He swooped and soared. His sharp claws almost clutched the small bird. The bird quickly swerved down to the ground and turned himself into an antelope. He leaped and sprang and dashed away. The hawk swooped down and turned himself into a wolf. He loped after the antelope, his jaws drooling for a fine meal. The antelope could feel the wolf's hot breath on his neck and knew that he was lost. In desperation he turned back into a man and pleaded, "Please do not kill me. You can have all your cows and goats back!"

The wolf turned into the magician and said, "Give me back the charm and all of your goats and cows. Then I will spare your life."

The older brother gave the magician the charm, the cows, and the goats. He lost his power and he lost his herd. A trickster must be careful who he tricks.

Duffy and the Devil

A FOLKTALE FROM ENGLAND

The autumn air was sweet with the smell of apples. It was cider pressing time on Squire Lovel's estate. He briskly galloped his horse past red dappled trees and jolly apple pickers, when suddenly he heard an angry quarrel coming from one of the cottages alongside the road.

"You're lazy and good for nothing!" scolded a woman in a shrill voice.

"I am not lazy!" a tearful girl spoke back. "I make the best meat pies in all of Cornwall!"

Squire Lovel rode to the cottage and quieted the argument. He asked the rosy-cheeked maiden, "Can you spin and knit? You seem unhappy here. Perhaps you'd prefer to work at my manor house."

"Well, sir, my name is Duffy," she said, dabbing her eyes with her apron. "I make the best meat pies in all of Cornwall, and I'd be happy to work for you if you'd have me."

"Come along then, you're hired," he said, helping her up behind him on the horse. "You'll soon be in the finest house around!"

"Good riddance!" shouted her old mistress, but Duffy's ears were listening only to the Squire, who bragged all the way home about his elegant abode.

When at last they entered the Squire's manor house, Duffy's high spirits fell. Clouds of dust rose up around her feet as she made her way through the clutter on the floor. When the Squire led her to the attic, she saw an old spinning wheel covered with cobwebs, and unspun fleece piled to the ceiling.

"As you can see, Duffy, no spinning's been done here for a while," said the

Squire. "I'll need some socks first. My toes are poking through. And I'll need a new hunting jacket and pants."

Duffy anxiously thought, "I don't know the first thing about spinning!" But she said out loud, with a curtsy, "I'll see to it first thing in the morning, sir!"

At dawn, the Squire went hunting. Duffy eyed the mess about her. She moved a bit of clutter and swept a few sweeps. Rolling clouds of dust floated up only to settle somewhere else. She sighed, and spent the rest of the day in the kitchen making meat pies, for that's what she liked to do best.

When the Squire returned home that evening, the meat pies smelled so delicious, he hardly remembered about the socks he needed until after supper. Happily patting his stomach he said, "I hope your spinning and knitting are as fine as your pies, Duffy."

"I haven't quite gotten to the attic, sir—maybe tomorrow," she mumbled.

The next day, once again, Duffy spent the day in the kitchen making pies. The Squire was pleased with his supper after a long day hunting, but seeing no spinning or knitting done, sorely complained, "My feet need warm socks, Duffy!"

"I'll go up to the attic this instant, Squire Lovel," she said to calm him.

The attic was a musty smelling place. Duffy eyed the piles of fleece and the spinning wheel. She stamped her foot and muttered out loud, "Oh, the devil can spin and knit for this messy old Squire for all I care!"

Suddenly Duffy heard a raspy laugh behind her. She turned to see an impish, pointy featured man, who said, with a devilish grin, "Duffy, my dear, I'll do all the spinning and knitting you can wish for. But, at the end of three years, you'll have to come away with me unless," he said, twirling his tail, "you can guess my name. You can have as many tries as you like."

"Well," considered Duffy, "in three years it will be easy enough to discover his name. In the meantime, all my woolen work will be done for me!" She agreed to the bargain.

The next morning Duffy found a fine pair of woolen socks waiting for her in the attic. Duffy brought them to the Squire, who was so pleased he went to church with his pants rolled up to his knees to show them off.

"And you should taste her meat pies!" he bragged to everyone.

After that, each day, Duffy wished for all kinds of interesting spun, knitted, and woven things. Britches, shirts, coats, and blankets all appeared with the help of the impish little man, who said, "No!" with glee, to every name she tried.

The Squire bragged often about Duffy's cooking and spinning. Before long, each night, there was a different young man sitting in the chimney corner come to court Duffy. The Squire was alarmed that he might lose his prize housekeeper to a suitor! So one day he said to Duffy, "Will you marry me?"

"Imagine a peasant girl like me," thought Duffy, "becoming Lady Lovel!" She agreed to become the Squire's wife. However, after the wedding, nothing much changed in her life except her name. The Squire spent all of his time out hunting and was content as long as he had his meat pies and warm socks.

Duffy soon became lonely and, for company, she went to the gristmill every morning to watch the women gather on the green. They danced and sang while their flour was being ground. Old Bet, the miller's wife, kept time for their dances on a drum made of a sieve covered by a sheepskin.

"Join in the dance, Duffy," Old Bet hollered. She often wondered how Duffy had so much free time every day and yet managed to produce such an abundance of fine woolen goods. Old Bet was a witch and soon guessed who was helping Duffy.

Three years passed quickly, and one day Duffy pounded anxiously on the gristmill door. "Old Bet," she pleaded, "please help me. You're the only one who might understand. I've made a frightful bargain. I'm going to have to spend eternity with an evil imp, for I cannot guess his name." She sobbed and buried her face in her hands.

Old Bet felt sorry for Duffy, and opening the mill door, she said, "Poor lass, when you can name your fear, it does not have power over you. I'll help you to be free of that imp if you promise never to make lazy bargains with the likes of him again."

"Never!" said Duffy, wiping her tears.

"Very well," said Old Bet, "Tonight is the full moon. Bring a jug of the

Squire's strongest applejack and meet me at sunset. Every sprite, fairy, hobgoblin and imp will come out to watch the witches dancing in the cavern."

At sundown, Duffy was at the mill with a large clay jug. Old Bet flung on a warm, red cape, took her drum and the jug of applejack and set out for the cave, with Duffy scampering after.

"Hide in the brambles and keep your ears and eyes open!" Old Bet cautioned.

Shivering from the damp and cold, Duffy hid herself behind the bushes and watched as the witches gathered and danced their strange dance around the blue flame of the fire that leaped almost to the ceiling of the cavern. Old Bet beat the drum to keep time for the dance. Sure enough, one by one, every sprite, pixie, fairy, and hobgoblin came out to watch, and one by one they joined in. Among them, Duffy saw the imp! Every time he came 'round the circle of the dance, Old Bet handed him the jug of applejack. He kept taking swigs until, finally, he became so tipsy and gleeful he began to swing his forked tail and sing a drunken song:

> *"Duffy, my lady, it's you I'll claim.*
> *Duffy, you'll never guess my name.*
> *I'll take you away and I'll never stop.*
> *I'm terrible, I terrify, I'm TERRYTOP!"*

Duffy's heart leaped to her throat. She whispered to herself, "Terrytop!"

Suddenly, just as she rose to leave, Duffy heard galloping and the baying of hounds. There was Squire Lovel and his dogs charging after a hare! But as the dogs approached the cave, they turned and ran off yelping, with their tails between their legs. The Squire pulled up his horse's reins and saw the great blue flame of the fire. He heard the drumming and saw the dance. He came closer and closer and closer. Finally, unable to hide himself any longer, he jumped into the circle with a heave and a ho! The witches rose up and chased him across the moor with the imps, sprites and fairies flying after. Squire Lovel barely got home with his breath.

He burst in the door to find Duffy at the stove. "What an adventure I've had!" he gasped. "There were witches, sprites, pixies and hobgoblins dancing around a fire! They were so angry when I joined in they chased me home! I felt like the hare I'd been hunting!"

"I hope they don't cause us any mischief," said Duffy, stirring up both the stew and the Squire's superstitions. "Strange things can happen when you disturb the goblins."

"I prefer not to think about goblins when there's a fine supper to be had," said the Squire with a shudder. He sniffed the pot hungrily and said, "I'll be back to eat as soon as I fetch my runaway dogs." Out he went into the night.

Swift as a sparrow, Duffy was in the attic. Sure enough the imp was there too, laughing wickedly.

"Duffy, oh Duffy, it's you I'll claim.
Duffy, you'll never guess my name!
Three more times, you may try,
then Duffy my dear,
off we'll fly!"

Duffy trembled as she asked, "Is your name Lucifer?"

"No, that's my uncle," he replied tartly.

"Beelzebub?" she whispered, barely able to speak.

"No! No! No! Just a cousin! Soon you'll be mine, mine, mine!" he taunted. "Just one more guess …"

"If I am correct, don't deny it," she blurted. "You are Terrytop!"

He raged and rasped, "How did you guess?!" He stamped his foot and disappeared in a puff of sulfur and smoke, howling, "You'll not keep a bit of my magic!"

When he vanished, every single thing he had spun or knitted for three years turned to ashes where it lay.

It was a bitter, cold night and the Squire was out riding on the moor … The first thing to go were his socks. Then his shirt, his coat, his pants, and in a snap, his woolen underwear disappeared.

When he came in the door, blue as ice, he stood with only his leather vest and riding boots on, saying, "Duffy, the strangest thing has happened."

"So I see," she gasped. "The same thing has happened here! Every bit of spinning and weaving I've done for three years has vanished. Some terrible evil is at hand and I think it is caused by the goblins you disturbed at their dance!"

"Could be," exclaimed the Squire, shivering and warming himself by the fire. "They certainly were angry! Well, you'll just have to get busy and make some more warm woolen things."

"I can't ..." Duffy said quickly. "I mean ... it probably wouldn't do any good." Thinking fast, she added, "What if the mischief at hand is a spell cast on anything I make for you! All my hard work might disappear when you'd least expect it! We can't take a chance! Imagine ... One day you'll be bowing before the Lords and Ladies at the royal court in your finest woolen clothes, and suddenly your suit will vanish! Or, what if, on a cold winter night, all our blankets disappear from our bed and we freeze in our sleep?"

Squire Lovel shivered and said, "That would never do. Perhaps it would be best for you not to do any more spinning, weaving, and knitting."

From that day on, village weavers made all the woolen goods used at the manor house. In time, Duffy and the Squire grew to love each other dearly. The Squire hunted happily each day and Duffy spent her afternoons doing just what she liked to do best ... making meat pies.

The Golden Touch

As King Midas walked into his royal rose garden, he stumbled over a strange creature sleeping in a flower bed. The top half of the odd looking visitor was human, but his bottom half was covered with gray hair, had a tail and hooves, and looked very much like a goat.

"Who are you?" Midas asked. But the creature did not stir. Concerned, Midas carried him to the court physician, saying, "This stranger seems ill. See to it that he is cared for kindly, until he is well again."

Thinking no more about the unusual guest, Midas retired to his throne room. Suddenly, before him appeared a great cloud and out of the billowing mist stepped a tall, beautiful man. Around his head he wore a wreath of grapes and in his hand he held a bunch of grapes. The man bowed and said, "I am Dionysus, God of Wine. I have come down from cloud-shrouded Mount Olympus, where I live with many powerful gods and goddesses, to thank you. The strange creature you helped today was a friend of mine, a satyr named Silenus. In return for your kind deed I will grant you one wish."

"A wish!" exclaimed King Midas in amazement, "I must consider this deeply …" His eyes brightened and he said, "My two greatest loves are my young daughter and the glistening color of pure gold. The more gold I have, the more I want. I can never have enough. I wish that anything I touch will turn to gold."

"Are you certain?" Dionysus asked in disbelief. "Why wish a curse upon yourself?"

"How could the touch of gold be anything but a blessing? Gold is as

dear to me as life itself. Just think of all I could buy for my beloved little daughter. I've made my wish!" said Midas defiantly.

"So be it," said Dionysus and vanished.

Midas felt an odd shudder come over him and wondered if his wish had been granted. He rushed out into his garden and went to a fig tree that was filled with ripe fruit. He touched a fig and it began to gleam and glow. He touched another, and another. Soon the tree hung heavy with golden orbs.

"The richest King in the world should have a golden throne!" shouted Midas, celebrating himself. He walked proudly into his throne room and went to his regal chair. One finger outstretched, he touched his throne. It turned to gold and the room grew bright with its glow.

"I am the richest King on Earth! I should have a feast to celebrate endless wealth! Servants!" Midas commanded, "I am very hungry. Bring me the finest meal!"

Servants hurried toward him with great trays of sumptuous food. Midas' mouth watered as he selected a tasty morsel. But when he picked it up with his fingers, it turned to gold before reaching his lips. His stomach growled as he impatiently touched another delectable treat. He reached again and again, but each bite of food he touched turned to gold!

"If I can't eat to ease my hunger, I shall drink to quench my thirst," He said. "Bring me a goblet of wine!"

Servants brought him a goblet filled with wine. But when Midas brought the goblet to his lips he saw that the wine, too, had turned to gold.

Horrified, Midas wailed, "Is this why Dionysus called the touch of gold a curse? I am hungry and I cannot eat! I'll be the richest man in all the world to die of hunger and thirst!"

At that moment, into the throne room came King Midas' young daughter, whom he loved dearly. When she saw her father so upset, she ran to him with her arms outstretched to hug and comfort him. He saw her running towards him and stretched out his hands to stop her from touching him, shouting "Stay back! Don't touch m—"

But alas, his fingers brushed against her and there before him stood his beloved daughter with her small arms outstretched. She was solid gold!

Midas clutched his hands and wept with grief, "What have I done! All the gold in the world cannot replace my daughter!"

As he wiped the tears from his eyes … his tears too turned to gold. "I was a fool to value gold over life itself," he wailed. "Gold cannot feed the belly or the heart. I wish this wretched curse could be washed away!"

Once again, the cloud appeared in the throne room and Dionysus stood before King Midas.

"Since you now regret your first foolish wish," said Dionysus, "I will grant your second. Go quickly to the river Pactolus at the edge of your Kingdom and wash yourself in its waters."

Like a madman, wild with grief, Midas ran from the palace to the river. He plunged into the water and washed and wept. As his tears flowed, they mingled with the river. The sand on the river bottom began to gleam. His daughter's golden form returned to human flesh as the sand on the riverbanks began to glow.

. . . .

Some people, who walk along certain riverbanks today, point to glittering sand and say, "The shiny sand on the bottom of this river is just fool's gold, or pyrite."

"No!" say others, "It might be real! Remember the old tale? This could be the very place where King Midas, so long ago, washed away the curse of the golden touch with his own tears."

The Contrary Fairy

A FOLKTALE FROM FRENCH CANADA

*L*ong ago and far away, there were two peaceful kingdoms nestled side by side. Celebration filled the air in one of the kingdoms, for the Queen had given birth to a daughter. People sang and danced in the streets to welcome the little Princess. The royal birthday party was a sumptuous feast, and everyone in the kingdom came with gifts and blessings.

L'Esprit de Joie, the Pleasant Fairy, arrived in a tiny chariot drawn aloft by silver dragonflies. For her gift, she gave the Princess a blessing, "Wherever you go, may flowers bloom and trees bear ripe fruit."

All the merriment and joyous singing roused Misérable, the Contrary Fairy, from her hole. No one knew exactly where she lived. She shunned people and especially avoided happy occasions. She was so wretched a creature that she could not bear anyone else's happiness. Like an insect sensing food, she felt the merriment and it disgusted her. She climbed into her coach drawn by six black-winged cats and soared off to discover who had disturbed her misery with the sound of laughter.

She flew over the palace just in time to hear the Pleasant Fairy speak her happy blessing over the princess. Misérable frowned a hideous crack of a smile and muttered wickedly, "We'll see about that!" Then, unable to bear the joviality a moment longer, she flew off to her dank, hidden dwelling.

Shortly thereafter, the Queen of the other kingdom gave birth to a son. Once again merriment filled the air. At his birthday celebration, L'Esprit de Joie arrived in her tiny chariot drawn by silver dragonflies and gave the Queen a gift for the Prince. She whispered into the Queen's ear, "I fear there is trouble

ahead for your son. Take this magic ring and give it to him when he's old enough to wear it. It is the Ring of Deliverance." Then she turned to the Prince and offered her blessing, "May you grow to be kind and well loved…"

The singing and dancing at the party again roused Misérable, the Contrary Fairy, who ranted, "Who has disturbed my wretchedness?" Flying out of her hole in a coach drawn by black-winged cats, she soared over the celebration. She arrived just in time to hear L'Esprit de Joie bless the Prince, "May you live in happiness."

Misérable's eyes squinted into two knife-edged slits. She puckered her lips so tightly she looked as if she'd been sucking lemons. She muttered bitterly, "We'll see about that," and flew swiftly back to her hole.

Years passed and the Prince and Princess grew up and fell in love. To everyone's delight, there was to be a royal wedding which would unite not only the happy couple, but the kingdoms as well.

Wedding preparations started months before the event. People planted flowers and painted and primped their houses. Colorful banners flew from rooftop and tower. Everyone began stitching party clothes. People sang and danced for the joy of love. None were happier than the starry-eyed Prince and Princess who walked through the countryside, hand in hand, speaking affectionately of their future.

One day the Princess said, as she strolled with the Prince, "I must return to my palace. The royal seamstress has just finished sewing my wedding gown and I must try it on."

The Prince sighed wistfully, "Then if we are to part, I will pick some flowers for you in the field."

Meanwhile, the abundant love and joy in the air roused Misérable, the Contrary Fairy, from her dark hole. Black-winged cats drew her coach out of the dismal solitude to investigate. As she hovered over the kingdoms, she saw the wedding preparations, she heard the love songs, and then, to her utter dismay, she saw the betrothed couple kissing goodbye. She shrieked, "I can't stomach this obnoxious happiness. It makes me sick. I must stop it once and for all."

Misérable hid behind a dark cloud until the Princess returned to the palace. Unaware of any danger, the Princess danced into her room and tried on the silken wedding gown. Her handmaidens scurried about, lacing and buttoning, until the Princess stood admiring herself in the chamber mirror. As she gazed at the reflection of happiness that she saw in the glass, a dark cloud wafted silently in through the window and enveloped the Princess. Before anyone could blink or shout, the Princess was gone.

Misérable, the Contrary Fairy, had seized the Princess, whisked her deep into the woods, and set her down in a crude cottage with a dead tree by its door. A twisted thorny hedge surrounded the cottage. The hedge grew so tall and prickly it would allow no one to go in or out. With a cackle and a snort, Misérable cursed as she flew off, "And here you'll stay until you are as wretched as I am!"

The Princess blinked in dismay at her horrid surroundings. She walked to the dead cherry tree and was suddenly quite hungry. In a moment the cherry tree burst into bloom and then hung heavy with ripe juicy cherries. Red roses blossomed on the tall wall of thorn briars. The Pleasant Fairy's wish for the Princess, "May flowers bloom and fruit trees bear ripe fruit," had taken hold. The Princess plucked some cherries and munched upon them as she pondered how to escape.

Meanwhile, as the Prince was collecting wildflowers for the Princess, Misérable, the Contrary Fairy, flew over him and said,

> *"You will smile no more to torment me.*
> *A small blue fox is what you'll be."*

A clap of thunder rumbled across the sky, and the Prince suddenly felt his hands change into paws. His face lengthened, his teeth grew sharp. His clothes disappeared and blue-gray fur covered his body. He slunk into the woods, dragging a long tail behind him.

Misérable, the Contrary Fairy, was pleased with her handiwork for only a brief moment. She despised happiness, even her own. Her sly grin strained her face until it ached and she grumbled as she flew away to her hole, "Now I can be unhappy without anyone annoying me with joy."

The blue fox ran wildly through the woods until, by chance, he came upon the wall of briars covered with roses. He poked his face through a small space near the ground. "It's the Princess!" he thought with alarm when he saw her picking cherries. Squeezing through the opening, he sat motionless as he stared at his love. He felt that surely his heart would break. "What misery," he thought, "my own true love stands before me and I cannot speak my feelings to her."

The Princess noticed the blue fox staring at her and said, "Do not be afraid of me. I will not hurt you. Come and be my company in this wretched captivity."

The fox approached slowly. The Princess reached down and stroked his head. Her hand's warm touch was more than the fox could bear. "She does not recognize me and I am powerless to tell her who I am," he thought, his heart heavy with sorrow. He turned and in despair crept back through the hole into the woods. He ran until he was panting and exhausted. Then he curled himself up beneath a tree and raged at the prison his fox's body had become.

The King and the Queen of each kingdom were frantic with worry. The Prince and Princess had mysteriously vanished and no one could find them. L'Esprit de Joie, the Pleasant Fairy, arrived to offer her help. She asked the Prince's mother, "Was your son wearing the Ring of Deliverance?"

"No," gasped the Queen, "I completely forgot about it. The day you gave it to him, I stored it safely away in my jewelry box." She quickly retrieved it and gave it to L'Esprit de Joie, who sped off to search for the couple.

The Pleasant Fairy's tiny chariot drawn by silver dragonflies darted about the kingdom looking for clues. As she flew over the fields at the edge of the forest, she looked down and noticed freshly picked wildflowers strewn over the ground. Human tracks disappeared suddenly and fox tracks led into the woods. L'Esprit de Joie followed the tracks until she heard a pitiful whining. "Something is hurt," she said out loud. Approaching the sound she saw the sad blue fox. She recognized his eyes and exclaimed, "Prince! It is you! I have your Ring of Deliverance." Then she sighed as she looked at his paws. "But it won't do you much good without fingers."

The fox's eyes brightened as he moved close to the fairy and opened his mouth. "Oh," she said, understanding, "You want to carry it on your tongue." The moment she placed the Ring in the fox's mouth, he dashed off deep into the forest. L'Esprit de Joie excitedly followed close behind. When they arrived at the tall briar, the Pleasant Fairy peeked between the roses and sharp thorns. She saw the captive Princess weeping and said, "This is the horrible work of Misérable, the Contrary Fairy. My birthday blessing has already helped the Princess a bit, but I am not powerful enough to free her from this prison of thorns."

The fox crouched low and, disregarding the stinging scratch of the sharp thorns, he squeezed through the opening once again. When the Princess saw him she smiled through her tears and welcomed him with a pat on his snout. "Hello," she said, "I am so lonely. Come and sit beside me." The Princess spread her silken gown around her and sat on the ground stroking the blue fox. "I was about to marry my beloved Prince," she said, "and now I am kept away from my love. I think that my heart shall break."

The fox opened his mouth and she saw the Ring. "What is this?" she asked, taking the Ring in her hand. "You want to marry me," she smiled. "Well then, let's pretend that you are my Prince. Yes, dear one, I will marry you and love you until we are old and gray." She slipped the Ring on her finger.

A great rush of sound made the Princess close her eyes. When she opened them again, the cottage was gone, the thorny rose briars had vanished, and before her stood her Prince. They embraced and, with tears of joy, returned to their parents. The wedding took place that evening and endless fireworks lit up the starry sky.

Misérable, the Contrary Fairy, was having a nightmare when the celebration reached its height and woke her up. "Not again!" she screeched. "I will destroy this joy once and for all. How dare they sing and dance when I want to be depressed." She flew out of her hole and zoomed over the joyous wedding celebration, ranting and rasping, "This is disgusting, obnoxious, and absolutely hideous. I won't stand for it!" She worked herself into such a hateful frenzy that she exploded with rage. Her angry sparks mingled with the fireworks and, fortunately for the happy Prince and Princess, Misérable was never seen again.

Drakestail

Once upon a time in France there lived a wicked king. He often made promises and then promptly forgot them. Once he borrowed money from a rich duck named Drakestail. With much pomp and ceremony, the King promised to pay back the loan. Rarely good to his word, however, the King considered the money his own.

Drakestail was infuriated when the King did not return the money. He paced in his parlor and muttered, "A good king should always keep his word! I am going to the palace this afternoon and demand my money back."

Drakestail set off down the road singing …

> *"I want my money back,*
> *I want it today!*
> *Donnez-moi de l'argent!*
> *S'il vous plait!"*

As he marched along to his tune, Drakestail came upon his friend, Fox. "Bonjour. Comment allez-vous? Good day. How are you?" asked Fox.

Drakestail replied, "I am quite upset! I am going to visit the King to tell him he must keep his word and repay his debt to me."

Fox said, "The King is wicked. He may not be pleased with your demand. Can I come too? Perhaps there's something I can do. One can never have enough friends!"

Drakestail replied, "Then jump into my magic gizzard." Drakestail had the unusual ability to shrink anything to a size that would fit in his throat.

Pooof! Fox shrank until he was the size of a barley seed, and into

Draketail's throat he went.

Drakestail continued singing down the road ...

"I want my money back,
I want it today!
Donnez-moi de l'argent!
S'il vous plait!"

Farther along Drakestail met his friends, Ladder and River. "Where are you going in such a rush?" they asked.

Drakestail replied, "I am going to the palace of the wicked King to demand my money back."

Ladder and River said, "Can we come too? Perhaps there's something we can do. One can never have enough friends!"

"I agree," said Drakestail. "Jump into my magic gizzard."

Pooof! Ladder became the size of a grain of rice. River was as small as a drop. Into Drakestail's throat they went.

Drakestail continued along, singing,

"I want my money back,
I want it today!
Donnez-moi de l'argent!
S'il vous plait!"

Drakestail met one last friend, Wasp. "Can *bzzz*, I *bzzz* come too?" asked Wasp. "Perhaps there is *bzzz* something I could *bzzz* do for *bzzz* you."

And poof! Wasp was riding along, the size of a millet seed, in Drakestail's magic throat.

At last Drakestail arrived at the Palace and knocked loudly on the door. "Give me my money back!" the duck shouted.

The King was in the throne room when he heard Drakestail's voice. He called for the Guards and said, "Throw that duck in the chicken house! The chickens will peck him 'til he bleeds!"

The Guards threw Drakestail into the chicken house. When the chickens saw a duck in their midst they charged at him and started pecking!

Drakestail called for the aid of his friend, Fox. In a blink, Fox jumped out of Drakestail's gizzard and chased away the chickens. Drakestail went back to the gate. "Give me my money back!" he shouted.

The wicked King heard Drakestail again. He called to the Guards, "Throw that duck into a deep dry well!"

Cast to the bottom of the well, Drakestail called for the aid of his friend, Ladder. Ladder jumped out of the magic gizzard, and up out of the well Drakestail climbed.

Angrier than ever, Drakestail went back to the gate. "Give me my money back!" he shouted.

The wicked King told the Guards, "Get rid of him once and for all! Throw him into the royal furnace!"

And they did!

As the flames licked at his feathers, Drakestail called for his friend, River. River washed the fire out! Drakestail went back to the gate and shouted even louder, "Give me my money back!"

The King couldn't believe his ears. "Still alive!" Furious, he hollered to his Guards, "Bring that duck to me. I'm going to sit on him and squash him flat!"

The King was a huge man. He put Drakestail on the royal chair and sat on him to squash him. The King flattened Drakestail until he gasped for breath. Just then, the duck remembered one last friend. He called for the aid of Wasp. Wasp came out of Drakestail's magic gizzard and stung the King on his big round bottom. Wasp kept stinging until the King ran through the palace door, down the royal road, and across the wide countryside. For all I know, that wicked King is still running.

Meanwhile, Drakestail sat up on the throne and fluffed his feathers. He decided to take the throne for himself.

Drakestail became a noble King,
whose praises still are heard.
He always kept his friends,
but above all kept his word.

The Mouse Bride

A FOLKTALE FROM FINLAND

*L*ong ago, when the world was filled with wonder, there was a farmer who had three sons. The two older sons took pleasure in teasing their youngest brother, who was so kindhearted he could not even sweep a spider from the cobwebs in the corner.

Now one day the farmer brought his sons to a field where three trees stood. "It is time for you to be wed," he said. "Each of you must cut down a sapling. When it falls, walk forward in the direction it points, and you will find your sweetheart."

The oldest son cut the largest sapling and it fell pointing north. "What luck!" he shouted, "I know of a fine maiden who lives in a house just north of here. I will go and ask for her hand in marriage."

The next oldest son cut a sapling and it fell pointing south. "I too shall live in happiness," said the second son, "for there is a delightful young woman who lives in a house just south of here. I will go and ask her to be my bride!"

But when the youngest son cut his sapling, it pointed towards the forest where there were no houses at all.

"You'll find a pointy-eared sweetheart with sharp teeth in that forest," laughed his two brothers.

"I will trust fate and my chances," said the youngest son. He carved a beautiful walking stick from the tree and set off in the direction of the woods.

The young man had not gone far into the forest when he came upon a cottage made of gray logs. He knocked on the door. A pleasant voice said, "Enter, please."

When he walked inside, he looked everywhere but saw no one.

"Here I am!" said the voice, "I am so glad to have company. I have been very lonely."

The young man stared in amazement. There on the table was a dainty blue-eyed mouse with its gray fur as sleek as velvet.

"You can speak!" the young man said.

"Certainly I can speak, but I prefer to sing," she said gaily, and she began a lively tune. The young man applauded her song, amazed. Then she curtsied and asked, "What brings you here?"

"I am searching for a sweetheart," he replied.

"Well then, how about me?" said the mouse.

"You are not exactly the type of sweetheart I was seeking," said the young man politely as he turned to leave.

"Oh," she sighed, "I am sad to hear that, for I have longed to meet someone just like you." She began such an enchanting love song, the young man stood motionless at the door.

"Please don't stop," he pleaded when she finished her song. "I want that song to go on and on ... Strange as it seems, perhaps you could be my sweetheart."

"Then come to visit me at this time tomorrow," she said with a smile and a twitch of her silken whiskers.

"I promise I will return," said the young man as he left. And all the way home, his heart quickened as he thought about the mouse and her beautiful song.

When he arrived at the farm that evening his two brothers were bragging to their father.

"The woman I met has beautiful rosy cheeks," said the oldest son.

"The lovely maiden I met," bragged the next oldest son, "is the fairest in the countryside. Her hair is as black as a raven's wing."

But they teased the youngest brother before he could speak a word, saying, "Who could you find in the woods but a pointy-eared, sharp-toothed beast!"

"I met the most enchanting singer," said the lad hesitantly, "and I cannot stop thinking about her. She has a captivating voice, sky-blue eyes, a beautiful smile, and she dresses in the very finest gray velvet. She even invited me to return tomorrow!"

"A princess no doubt!" the brothers shouted sarcastically. "He is making this up! Who could love him?"

"Congratulations to each of you on meeting sweethearts," said their father. "But attractive looks alone do not make for a happy hearth. Tomorrow, I should like to see the kind of bread your sweethearts bake."

The next morning, the youngest son set out at dawn. When he arrived at the cottage the mouse greeted him eagerly, saying, "I am delighted that you have kept your promise to return!"

The lad blushed with embarrassment and said, "I told my father and brothers that ever since we met, I have not been able to stop thinking about you. But I did not tell them that you are a mouse! Now my father would like to see the kind of bread you bake! Oh," he moaned, "my cruel brothers will certainly ridicule me when I arrive home tonight empty-handed!"

"I cannot bear to think of them mocking you! You will not go home empty-handed!" said the mouse. "Of course I can bake bread!" She clapped her paws and one hundred gray mice appeared as she commanded, "Bring me the finest grains of wheat from the field!"

Fascinated, the young man stayed all day watching the marvelous effort as the little mouse directed the baking of a fine loaf of wheaten bread. She sang as she worked and enraptured the young man's ears with her music. The afternoon passed so quickly with their cheerful conversation and laughter, the young man hardly noticed that the sun was setting.

"I must hurry and leave," he said.

"Please take this loaf as a gift to your father," said the mouse, waving him goodbye. "I hope that you will come again tomorrow."

"Of course I'll return," assured the young man, "I would rather be here than anywhere else." He traveled back home with the loaf under his arm.

That night around the dinner table, the oldest brother proudly handed the farmer a loaf of rye bread made by his sweetheart and boasted, "See how hearty and well-baked it is!"

The second oldest brother handed the farmer some barley bread made by his sweetheart and bragged, "My sweetheart's bread is crusty and healthy to eat!"

But when the youngest brother handed his father the fine loaf of wheaten bread the farmer exclaimed, "Wheat bread! Only the richest among us eat wheat bread!"

The two older brothers bickered over who was to get the biggest piece of wheat bread and said, as they stuffed their mouths, "But there's no house in that woods for miles! What kind of sweetheart could you have found?"

"One whose conversation can make me forget the time of day," replied the lad.

"I am pleased that your sweethearts bake such fine bread!" said the farmer. "Skillful hands add comfort to a home. Tomorrow, I should like to see the kind of cloth they can weave."

The next morning the lad set out again to visit the mouse in the woods.

"Come in!" said the little mouse when she heard him knock. She sang him a tune and a smile spread across his face.

"I wish you could weave as well as you bake and sing. But how could that be possible?" said the lad with a sigh. "My father would like to see the kind of cloth you make."

"Love makes everything possible," said the mouse, clapping her paws. Once again, one hundred mice appeared as she said, "Fetch me strands of the finest flax."

Each mouse quickly returned with one strand of flax. The little mouse spun the flax into thread on a tiny spinning wheel. The young man stared in amazement as she wove a fine piece of linen on a miniature loom. They kept company all afternoon, talking and laughing while she worked. The time sped by so quickly, the sun was setting before the young man realized it.

"It's done!" she finally said, folding the small patch of delicate cloth in a walnut shell. "Take it to your father as a gift and I do hope your heart brings you here tomorrow."

The lad left for home with the walnut shell tucked carefully in his pocket.

That night around the hearth fire, each brother brought forward the cloth made by their sweethearts.

"Here is some coarse but sturdy cotton made by my love," boasted the first brother proudly.

"Here is some cotton and linen weave made by my love, and it is fancier than yours!" bragged the second brother.

"Here is a walnut," said the youngest brother as his older brothers howled.

"He has no sweetheart! He's brought a forest nut instead of some cloth!" they squealed.

"Appearances can be deceptive," said the lad. "Open the nut, Father."

The two older brothers stopped laughing and gawked in silence as the farmer opened the shell and held up the fine web of linen. "I have never seen such delicate work," said the farmer, admiring the cloth. "Sons, I must meet your sweethearts! Bring them home tomorrow so that I may see your brides-to-be," he said.

The lad's face flushed red as he imagined himself presenting the little mouse to his father and brothers as his bride. "This is ridiculous!" he thought. "I cannot marry a mouse! I must seek deeper in the forest for a proper human sweetheart."

But in the morning, as the young man approached the cottage he could not resist stopping for a moment. He thought, "I will tell her politely that I won't be visiting anymore. I need to find one of my own kind. But then, surely I will hurt her feelings! She is the most delightful companion I've ever met. Oh, I have never been more confused!"

As he nervously stood at the cottage door wondering what to do, the little mouse called out, "Welcome! Come in! I have composed a love song for you!"

The moment he entered the room she began to sing her beautiful song. His heart swelled with joy and every doubt he had about presenting her to his family disappeared with the first tones of her sweet voice.

"My Father wishes to meet you," he simply said. "Please come with me to visit him."

"Very well, I shall travel in the finest style!" replied the mouse.

She clapped her paws and six black mice appeared, pulling a tiny coach made of a chestnut burr with a toadstool for a canopy.

The mouse, regal as a queen, climbed into the coach. With the youngest son walking alongside, they set out for his home.

When they arrived at the river, a hunter passed them on the bridge. He looked down at the mouse, coach, and six and exclaimed, "Ho! What is this! A pack of vile rodents! I hate rats."

"If you please, sir," said the lad, "these are not vile rodents. I'll not allow you to call them so!"

"I've killed every rodent that has crossed my path!" said the bully, looming dangerously over the lad.

"Open your eyes and look more carefully," said the young man bravely. "Here before you rides the most delightful creature one could chance to meet."

"Disgusting rats!" glowered the man and with his heavy boot he kicked the coach and six into the swift water below the bridge!

"Heartless cruel man!" screamed the lad as he jumped into the river to save the mouse.

"I've rid the world of some useless pests!" the hunter shouted and continued on his way.

The lad desperately tried to reach the sinking coach. But as the raging water swirled around the little mouse, she vanished in the rushing river.

Exhausted and almost drowned, the lad made his way to the riverbank. He climbed out of the water and wept. "Now that you are gone," he wailed, "I regret even one moment's doubt that you were indeed my true love."

Suddenly, with a great splash and spray of mist, out of the water came six black horses pulling a fine golden carriage. In the carriage was a beautiful woman with sparkling blue eyes, wearing a gray velvet gown.

"Who are you?" the lad asked, rubbing his eyes to be sure he was seeing clearly.

"Don't you recognize me?" she asked. Her lovely musical voice cheered his heart.

She explained, "I am a royal princess. A Lapland witch, jealous of my beauty, enchanted me to be a mouse until such time as a kindhearted man could truly love me for myself. You broke the spell when you risked your life and declared your love. I am your mouse bride if you will have me," she said with a shy smile.

"I loved you before when we were of different worlds." he said, "How could I love you less now?"

He climbed into the coach and together they rode to his father's house. His brothers tumbled over one another to greet the elegant guest at their gate. "But it's our brother!" they gawked as he stepped out of the coach holding the princess's hand.

After a day of celebration, the young man and the princess traveled back to the forest. Instead of finding the small cottage made of gray logs, they found a great gray stone castle filled with one hundred servants. And it was there that they dwelt in happiness for the rest of their lives.

The Pedlar of Swaffham

AN ENGLISH FOLKTALE

Once there was a poor pedlar who lived in the old English town of Swaffham. Every day he walked out of his cottage door, past the great oak tree that grew beside it, and sold wares from the knapsack he wore on his back. His little dog would follow, yipping at his heels. Everyone knew when the pedlar was coming for he sang …

"Knicknacks! Brick-a-Bracks! Fine and shiny things!"

Some days he sold enough to buy himself a loaf of bread for his dinner and a bone for his dog. But there were many nights when he went to sleep hungry.

One such hungry night, he had a dream. In the dream he heard a voice. It said,

"Go stand on London Bridge and you will hear good news."

In the morning, he remembered his dream. As he walked out of his cottage door, past the great oak tree that grew beside it, he wondered, "What could a dream like this mean?"

The next night, he had the same dream. Once again he heard the voice …

"Go stand on London Bridge and you will hear good news."

In the morning, he remembered the dream again. As he walked out of his cottage door, he leaned up against the oak tree and wondered, "What could a dream like this mean?"

On the third night, when he heard the voice again, he sat bolt upright in his bed and decided to go to London in the morning.

He set out at dawn, knapsack on his back, little dog at his heels. As he walked down the road with a skip and a whistle he sang a new song. He made it up as he went along.

"As foolish as it seems,
sometimes it's wise to follow your dreams.
Follow, follow your dreams, your dreams,
follow, follow your dreams."

He walked, and he walked, and he walked for a week. At last he arrived in the royal city of London. In these olden times, London Bridge was a great stone expanse with shops lining its sides. He went directly to the middle of the bridge and, just as the voice in the dream had instructed him, he and his little dog just stood there, waiting for good news.

He stood all day … He stood all night … He stood through the rain 'til the sun came out. No one stopped to speak to him.

Finally, a shopkeeper, who had been watching him the whole time, approached the pedlar and said, "Pardon me sir, but I have been watching you from my shop window for days now. I am curious to know what you are doing on London Bridge. You don't sell anything and I haven't seen you beg. Yet, you stand here day after day. What are you doing on London Bridge?"

The pedlar blushed and said, "I hardly know you to tell you such private things … but, then again … you are the first person to speak to me since I arrived in London. So, perhaps I will tell you … Sir, I had a strange dream for three nights. Each night I heard a voice which said, 'Go stand on London Bridge and you will hear good news.' Now I know this doesn't make much common sense, but sometimes common sense makes no sense at all. I am a man of feelings. I felt I should come and that is why I stand on London Bridge."

The shopkeeper began to laugh. He laughed so hard he had to hold his belly! He laughed so hard a crowd gathered to find out what was so funny …

"Listen to this!" he said to the crowd. "Here is the biggest fool you will ever meet. He is standing on London Bridge because he heard a voice in his dream!"

Everyone in the crowd began to point at the pedlar and call him a silly fool.

But the pedlar just stood there. When he didn't move, the shopkeeper, enjoying the taunting, drew the crowd in even tighter and said, "Ha! Following dreams? What a foolish man you are. I had a dream just last night. I dreamt of a place I've never even heard of ... Swaffham, I think it was ... I dreamt that if I dug in the ground in front of an oak tree that grew beside a poor pedlar's cottage I would find a treasure. Now do you think I would be foolish enough to leave my home and my work to follow some silly dream? Do yourself a favor, sir, and go back from where you came."

The pedlar's face spread wide with a smile. "I certainly will go back," he said and ran all the way home to Swaffham.

When he arrived at his cottage, he took a shovel and began to dig in the ground in front of the oak tree he knew so well. Sure enough, he found an iron box. When he pulled it up out of the hole and brushed away the soil, he saw that there were words inscribed on its lid which said,

Travel far,
travel wide,
the greatest treasure is deep inside ...

He opened the box and saw that it was filled with gold and jewels! He gave half of the treasure to the poor, for he himself had known hunger. And with the rest, he built a church which stands to this day, with a statue of the pedlar and his dog.

There was enough gold left over so that the pedlar and his dog lived comfortably all the days of their lives. As he walked down the road with a skip and a whistle, people often heard the pedlar singing ...

"As foolish as it seems,
sometimes it's wise to follow your dreams,
follow, follow your dreams, your dreams,
follow, follow your dreams."

The Boy Who Drew Cats

A FOLKTALE FROM JAPAN

◆◇ ◆◇ ◆◇ ◆◇ ◆◇

*L*ong ago in Japan, there was a farm boy who was a natural artist. Every moment he could spare from his chores, he drew cats, cats, cats.

Sleeping cats, creeping cats, stalking cats, walking cats, fighting cats, biting cats,
  quick,
    slick,
      curious,
        luxurious,
          cats!
Cat eyes, cat claws, cat thighs, cat paws,
Cats! Cats! Cats!

The boy's father was a hard-working farmer who complained, "Son, you creep away so often to draw cats, you've neglected your farm chores. You seem better suited to lift a paintbrush than a hoe. I will take you to the monastery at the top of the mountain where there is an old monk who can teach you to read and write. Perhaps then you can make some use of your brush strokes."

The boy was delighted. If I could read and write, he thought, I would write poems about cats!

He packed his best ink stone and his finest brush and set off with his father up the mountain.

The old monk who greeted them at the monastery gate welcomed the boy as a student. When they entered the temple, he gave the boy a sleeping mat and a rare old book to study.

"Care for this book well," he said. "It is a valuable treasure."

The boy admired the delicate brush strokes on the pages and then carefully put the book beside his sleeping mat, next to his best ink stone and brush.

Each day, the boy tried to concentrate on his lessons, but every time he noticed some empty space, such as a white wall, a rice paper screen, or the white edges around the writing in the old book … he could not help himself … He took out his ink stone and brushes and he drew cats, cats, cats …

Sleeping cats, creeping cats, stalking cats, walking cats, fighting cats, biting cats,
  quick,
    slick,
      curious,
        luxurious,
          cats!
Cat eyes, cat claws, cat thighs, cat paws,
Cats! Cats! Cats!

One night, the old monk discovered the cat drawings in the old book and exploded at the boy. "You must leave!" he raged. "You've drawn cats on every surface in this temple!"

But as he threw open the door and ordered the boy out, he considered for just a moment and said ominously, "Something lurks in the night. Be careful, or your heart will turn to stone with fright. Take this advice with you and go! Beware of large spaces and keep to small places."

The boy shuddered under the glare of the monk's stern gaze. He quickly packed his drawing tools, thanked the monk for his advice, and hurried out the door.

Night was falling as the boy started down the darkening road. After a while he stumbled upon a deserted temple. An eerie glow came from within its central hall. The boy cautiously entered and saw a huge empty space. Cobwebs hung everywhere.

He carefully eyed the edges of the room. Along all the walls were large, white rice paper screens. A smile spread over his face. He couldn't help himself. He took out his brush and paint and began to draw cats, cats, cats!

Sleeping cats, creeping cats, stalking cats, walking cats, fighting cats, biting cats,
  quick,
    slick,
      curious,
        luxurious,
          cats!
Cat eyes, cat claws, cat thighs, cat paws,
Cats! Cats! Cats!

He drew until he grew so tired he wanted to sleep. Suddenly, he realized that he was in a large space. He worried to himself, "the old monk told me to beware of large spaces." He noticed a small cabinet in the corner and decided, I'll sleep in that small place.

He opened the cabinet door, climbed in, and curled himself up like a cat. After a while he fell into a deep sleep.

During the night he was awakened by horrible sounds coming from the middle of the room ...
  Scratching ...
    hissing ...
      screeching ...
        growling ...
          Sounds of huge monsters prowling ....

The boy's heart was pounding but he didn't dare come out until the dawn.

At the first rays of morning light, he cautiously opened the cabinet door. In the middle of the temple floor, lying motionless in a pool of its own blood, he saw a huge rat goblin, the size of a cow.

That creature was coming to eat me! thought the trembling boy, as he crept out of the cabinet. *Who saved me? The old monk must be here!*

But, as he looked around he saw that no one was there ....

He glanced up at the white rice paper screens, and stared with amazement at his cat drawings. Every cat had a delicate line of rat goblin blood, dripping off the edge of its mouth and claws.

"My cats saved me!" he gasped.

At that moment the young boy knew, regardless of what anyone said, he would always draw cats!

The boy grew to be a man.

He became a legendary painter in Japan.

If you go there today,

people will show you his paintings and say,

at least once a day,

he drew cats, cats, cats ...

Sleeping cats, creeping cats, stalking cats, walking cats, fighting cats, biting cats,
    quick,
        slick,
            curious,
                luxurious,
                    cats!
Cat eyes, cat claws, cat thighs, cat paws,
Cats! Cats! Cats!

The Search for the Magic Lake

*L*ong ago, a powerful Inca ruler named Pachacuti governed a vast empire in Ecuador. His palace walls were covered with gold and glistened like the sun. But his mood was always dark and sorrowful. His only son, Topa, lay weak and dying. None of the court doctors could cure him. The Inca ruler grieved and went to the altar to pray. An eerie voice drifted out to him from the flames at the altar. "Your son must drink the waters of the Magic Lake that touches the sky," it said. "Fill the magic golden flask!"

The fire smoldered to embers and when it cooled, the golden flask was lying in the ashes.

Pachacuti was too old to travel to the end of the world to fill the flask with water from the Magic Lake. He announced, "I will give a great fortune to anyone who can bring water from the Magic Lake to the palace."

Two young men who lived on a farm in the valley heard about the reward. "Let us search for the Magic Lake," they said to each other. "If we find its healing waters, we will save our Prince and help our poor parents to live a comfortable life."

Their younger sister pleaded, "Let me come too!"

"No, stay here with our old parents," they said. "The journey will be too long and dangerous for you. We will return in time for the harvest."

Leaving their disappointed sister behind, the young men went in search of the Magic Lake. They traveled for months and still did not reach the end of the world, where the Magic Lake touches the sky.

"It is almost harvest time," said one son wearily. "Let us bring some

water from any lake we find along the way and go home. Surely the Emperor will reward us for our troubles."

The two young men delivered jars of ordinary water to the palace. Doctors brought the water to the Prince. He sipped the water, but lay as pale and weak as ever.

"This water could not be from the Magic Lake," said the court doctor. "They have lied about where they found it!"

The Emperor was furious at the deception. "Lying is a serious crime. Put these men in prison!" he cried. The two were dragged away and locked in a dungeon.

When news of their imprisonment reached home, their sister said, "I will seek the Magic Lake. Perhaps, if I find it, my brothers will be freed." She filled a small sack with roasted corn and brought a bottle of chicha, a corn mash drink. With her pet llama for company, she bravely set off.

They traveled a long way down the highway. By nightfall, the girl heard the sound of a hungry puma. Trembling with fright, she said, "Go home, dear llama, where you will be safe." She chased him back down the road. For safety, she climbed a tree. Nestled in the branches, she opened her bag of roasted corn. Three small birds landed beside her on the branch. Opening her hand, she let the birds peck the corn from her palm until they had eaten most of it. She drank her chicha and fell asleep.

As she slept, one bird said, "She will never reach the Magic Lake without some help."

Another added, "She fed us, so we should help her!"

When the girl heard these small voices, she opened her eyes. The birds fluttered to a branch in front of her face. "Take a feather from each of our wings. Make them into a fan and they will help you on your way."

Then each bird plucked a downy feather from under its wing. Taking the feathers from their beaks, she made a fan and tied it at the bottom with her hair ribbon.

"I wish I were at the Magic Lake," she sighed. Instantly a strong wind arose and whisked her out of the tree. She soared over the forest and gently landed in front of a lake so large its distant shore seemed to touch the sky.

"This must be the Magic Lake!" she cried. "I wish I had a jar that could carry the healing water."

No sooner did she say these words than a golden flask landed at her feet. Just as she leaned down to pick it up, she heard something scratching the sand behind her. She turned and saw an enormous, hairy-legged crab. "Leave the water alone!" it said.

The girl held the feather fan up to her mouth and the giant crab fell asleep.

She heard a great splash in the water and turned to see a giant alligator thrust his tail against the surface. "Leave the water alone!" it said.

She held up the fan and the alligator fell asleep and floated away.

Above her there was a strong wind. She looked up to see a huge winged serpent hissing, "SSSStay away! Leave the water alone!"

She held up her feather fan to her lips and the serpent descended onto the shoreline and fell asleep too.

As quickly as she could, she filled the golden flask. "I wish I were in the palace," she said.

When she blinked again, she was standing beside the sickly Prince, ashen pale on his bed. His father and mother wept over the lifeless body of their only son.

"I have brought the healing water of the Magic Lake," said the girl, holding up the golden flask.

She rushed to the Prince's side and let several drops moisten his lips. He began to stir. She lifted his head and poured a sip into his mouth. The blush of health spread over his face. He drank more and sat up with a smile.

"You have saved our son!" cried the Emperor Pachacuti. "Name anything you want as a reward."

"I desire only three things," said the girl. "First, I want my parents to have a comfortable farm and a herd of llamas, vicuñas, and alpacas."

"Done!" said the Emperor.

"Next," she said, "I want you to free my brothers. Surely they have learned their lesson and will never lie again. They were trying to help my parents."

"Done!" said the emperor.

"Lastly," she said, "I want these feathers returned to the birds who gave them to me. My mission is finished."

Before the emperor could speak, the feather fan rose up out of her hand. It floated across the room and vanished out the window.

"What can we give you for yourself?" asked the Emperor. "Please stay here with us and live in great riches."

"No," said the girl, "my greatest reward will be to see my family together again."

She returned home to discover that royal workers were already building a new house. Her parents rejoiced and her two brothers offered humble thanks as they lifted her high up onto their shoulders and danced about the farm.

The Olden Golden Goose

A Jataka Tale from India

A poor woman lived beside the river with her two daughters. The girls barely had enough to eat and their thin faces rarely smiled. The mother worried each day about how to find food for the family to eat.

One day a goose with magical golden feathers watched the woman and her daughters from behind some bushes. The bird pitied the family and waddled forward toward them. "Oh, look!" said one daughter, "a fat goose to eat!"

The girls caught the goose and carried it to their mother, but before she could make plans for the stew pot, the goose spoke. "Do not eat me!" it said. "Instead, pluck a single feather from my tail … Just *one*, and no more."

The mother jumped back upon hearing the goose speak. But one daughter carefully followed the goose's instructions and plucked a single feather from his tail. To everyone's delight, the feather turned to solid gold in the girl's fingers.

"Let me go," said the golden goose. "I will return and give you a single feather whenever you need more money. You will never again suffer as you do."

The daughter put the goose down and it flew away in a blink.

The family sold the golden feather at the marketplace and received enough money to fill their cooking pot with food. That night they ate until they were full. They slept like contented cats until morning.

After that, each day the goose returned and allowed the girls to pluck a single feather from its tail. The family was never hungry again.

One evening, the mother, who now had idle time to think of other things besides earning money, began to wonder. "What will we do if some day the golden goose does not return? We will be poor and hungry again."

These thoughts plagued her until she could think of nothing else.

"Daughters," she said finally, "the next time the golden goose comes to us, we must catch him and pluck out all of his feathers. Then we will have enough gold for a lifetime."

"But Mother," pleaded her daughters, "the goose will suffer without his feathers. He has always come when we needed him. Why doubt his generosity now?"

"I am only thinking of your well-being," said the mother, trying to make her daughters comply with her plot. "You must do as I say or someday you may find yourself hungry again."

The daughters refused to catch the goose the next time he visited. "You disobedient girls!" scolded the mother. "I will just have to do this myself."

The mother greedily chased the goose around the yard. At last she snatched the bird up in her hands and plucked out every feather. "I am doing this for you, daughters," she said. "The least you could do is help!"

The daughters watched and wept as feathers flew in every direction. Their mother stood with clumps of feathers in both hands, but they did not turn to gold. The goose had magical feathers indeed, but if they were plucked out against his will, they remained quite ordinary. The woman put the goose on the ground and it waddled away, shivering and miserable in its nakedness.

The daughters sadly covered the goose with blankets. In time its feathers grew back, white as snow. It flew away and never returned again.

The Firebird, the Horse of Power, and the Princess Vasilissa

A FOLKTALE FROM RUSSIA

*L*ong ago in Russia, there was a magical Horse of Power with fiery eyes, hooves of iron, and a strong, broad chest. The steed was wiser than most people, and always gave excellent advice to his riders.

One day, his master, a young warrior, galloped the Horse through a pine forest, scattering small animals and kicking up the underbrush. As he rode, the warrior noticed a golden feather lying in his path, and rearing back on the Horse's reins, he leaped down to reach for it.

The Horse of Power cautioned, "Leave the Firebird's golden feather where it lays!"

"If it is a golden feather from the Firebird," exclaimed the lad, "I must take it as a gift to the Tzar!"

"I warn you," said the Horse, "there is danger here."

"Nonsense!" said the warrior stubbornly. "The Tzar will be pleased to have such a rare treasure." He put the feather in his pocket and rode off to the palace.

The warrior presented the unusual feather to the Tzar. The ruler greedily smiled as he admired the gift and said, "Anyone who can bring me a feather from the Firebird can bring me the bird as well. Capture the Firebird or your head will no longer sit upon your shoulders."

The warrior returned to his Horse and said with a tremble, "Now that the Tzar has one golden feather, he wants the entire bird or I am to lose my head."

"I always offer good advice," muttered the Horse. "Tell the Tzar that you will bring him the bird if he spreads one hundred sacks of millet seed on a field in the moonlight."

This was done, and when the moon was high over the field, the warrior hid beside the Horse of Power, who grazed quietly. Suddenly there was a great burst of light and a swish of wind. With a wide swoop, the Firebird landed in the distance and began to peck at the seeds.

The Horse of Power and the warrior edged silently toward the bird. The Firebird was so busy eating, he did not notice their approach. The Horse stepped on the Firebird's tail. The warrior leaped onto the bird and with a struggle, the bird was tightly bound and draped over his shoulders like a golden cape. He jumped onto the Horse and rode swiftly to the palace.

The Tzar was delighted to see the Firebird before him. He smiled broadly and said, "Anyone who can capture the Firebird can bring me the Princess Vasilissa from the Land of Never. Go and return with the maiden or you will lose your head!"

The warrior went to his Horse of Power and moaned, "Now, surely, I will lose my life unless I find the distant Land of Never and bring the Princess Vasilissa to the Tzar."

"I will help you again," sighed the Horse, "for you are my master. First, go and ask the Tzar to give you tasty foods and a silver tent with a golden roof."

Once the warrior had the food and tent packed on the Horse's back, they galloped off to the Land of Never. On the shore of an azure lake, the warrior raised the tent and displayed the food and drink. In the distance, he heard a splash, and glancing across the water, he saw a young woman rowing a silver boat with golden oars. Boldly, she rowed to shore, climbed out of the boat, and approached the tent.

"I am Princess Vasilissa," she announced.

"Join me for some fine food," said the warrior.

The young woman was hungry and pleased with the invitation. The two sat eating and laughing until the warrior said, "Would you like to ride on my magic Horse?"

Her curiosity drew her to the huge Horse, and she and the warrior climbed up onto his back. In less than a wink they were in the throne room of the Tzar.

"Well done!" said the Tzar. "You have brought me my bride! Let the wedding take place at once."

The warrior was horrified at what he had unwittingly done. He rushed to rescue the Princess from the Tzar's guards, but they surrounded her with their swords and beat him back.

The Princess struggled to escape by delaying the wedding. "I cannot marry," she said firmly, "without my proper wedding gown ... It lies under a rock at the center of the ocean."

The Tzar turned to the warrior and said, "Since you have brought me the Princess Vasilissa, surely you can bring me her wedding gown from the bottom of the sea. I am losing my patience! Go and fetch it, or both you and the Princess will lose your heads!"

The warrior left the palace and said sadly to his Horse, "I am sinking in a sea of trouble. My heart aches for the trouble I have caused the Princess. Now we will both lose our heads, for I cannot possibly bring the gown from the bottom of the sea."

"Quickly climb on my back," commanded the Horse.

The Horse galloped off to the shallow rim of the sea where a giant lobster slowly crawled along the water's edge. The Horse of Power stepped on its tail and said, "Bring me Princess Vasilissa's wedding gown from under a rock at the bottom of the sea."

The lobster called all the crabs of the ocean to bring the wedding gown. Down, down, down the crabs went to a huge rock at the bottom of the sea. With their many claws they overturned the rock and floated the gown to the surface. Hundreds of crabs carried it to the warrior. He leaped onto the Horse, and with the dress flying behind him like a sparkling flag, he arrived at the Palace of the Tzar.

"Now," said the Tzar, "we can have the wedding immediately!"

"Not yet," said the Princess, delaying further. "I will not marry until you punish the warrior who lured me away from my lovely lake. Boil him in a cauldron of water."

"Anything to please you, my bride," said the Tzar wickedly. "Servants!" he called, "bring a huge pot of water to boil!"

The warrior trembled. "Please," he said, "before I die, at least allow me to bid goodbye to my faithful Horse."

"You may have your last request," said the Tzar.

The warrior walked to his Horse and whispered, "Goodbye, dear friend, for I will soon be dead. I am to be boiled alive by order of the woman I have wronged."

"She is not wicked," replied the Horse. "Trust that she has a plan and leap bravely into the pot."

The warrior humbly said, "You have always given me good advice, loyal friend. I will do as you say."

When the huge cauldron was boiling and the steam billowed upwards, the Princess said, "I must be certain that the water is hot enough." She walked to the pot and waived her hand over the cauldron's top. "Yes, it is ready," she said with a sly grin. "The warrior must jump in!"

Some say she had some magic *power* in her hand and others say she had some magic *powder* in her hand. But nevertheless, when the warrior leaped into the boiling water, it tickled and tossed him about. He bobbed, and laughed, and jumped out of the water, rosy-cheeked, refreshed and more youthful-looking than when he had jumped in.

Amazed at seeing such a miracle, the old Tzar exclaimed, "I am going to jump into that magic water and become young again too."

The Tzar was endlessly greedy and could not be stopped once he set his mind to something. He did just what the Princess had suspected he would do. He rushed to the cauldron, leaped in, and vanished in the bubbling brew.

Princess Vasilissa rose up upon the royal throne and declared herself ruler over the land. The warrior bowed humbly and vowed to serve her faithfully forever after, which he did, with his wise Horse by his side.

The Beggar King

Asmodeus, the powerful King of the Demons, stood in chains before King Solomon's throne. "Now that the construction of my temple is completed," King Solomon said, "Asmodeus, I will give you your freedom. But first, you must answer a question which has plagued me deeply. Often, as King, I am asked to be a wise judge. This is a difficult task. How can I truly know the difference between truth and illusion?"

Asmodeus, the King of the Demons, bowed low and said, "What is the difference between truth and illusion? Ahh ... This is a simple question to answer. But first, you must give me your ring."

King Solomon wore two rings. One was a ring inscribed with three Hebrew letters standing for the words THIS TOO SHALL PASS. He gave the ring to people who were having great difficulty in their lives. He also gave the ring to people who were experiencing great joy. This was not the ring that Asmodeus wanted. He pointed to King Solomon's sacred ring, inscribed with the unutterable name of The Most High upon it. King Solomon removed his holy ring and he gave it to the Demon King.

Asmodeus took the ring and threw it to the other side of the world. It landed in the middle of an ocean and sank to the bottom. Powerless before the Demon King, Solomon was lifted high into the air by Asmodeus and thrown to the other side of the world. He landed in the middle of a desert.

When he awoke, Solomon was no longer dressed in the royal robes of a king. He was dressed in the rags of a beggar. He told people, "I am a king ... a great king! I had a ring, a crown and a scepter."

People thought he was a mad beggar and called him "Liar! Impostor!"

Soon, Solomon stopped proclaiming himself a king and wandered until he found work. He became the cook's assistant in a fine palace. One day it came to pass that Solomon seasoned the King of the Palace's meal. When the King tasted his food he cried out at once, "Who has prepared this delicious dish? Bring the cook before me!"

The cook was brought before the King and admitted, "It was my assistant, Solomon, who seasoned the meal."

Solomon was brought before the King, and as he entered the throne room, the King's daughter Naamah saw Solomon. She fell in love with him and said to her father, "I will have no other man for my husband but the cook's assistant."

The King was enraged and had Solomon and Naamah cast out into the desert to die. They did not die, however. Solomon irrigated the land and he and Naamah planted fruit trees. They built a hut and lived together in the desert for twelve years. They had three children. And at night, Solomon slept the sleep of a man who had earned his rest. The heavy burden of being a wise king was no longer on his shoulders. He slept without care, weary only from the day's work. For the first time in his life, he was truly happy.

One day, as he was hoeing the garden with his children, Solomon noticed a dark cloud on the horizon. As it came closer and closer, he saw that it was not a cloud at all … It was a huge wave. The wave washed over the hut, smashing it! It circled around him. He clutched two of his children to his chest and in trying to reach for the third, all three were lost to him. He was engulfed, not only by his own tears, but by the blackness of the wave which surrounded him.

When the waters receded, so deep was his grief at the loss of his family, he was blinded by his tears. He did not even notice that he had also lost his freedom. Slavers had found him wandering, weeping. He was in chains, being led to the marketplace to be sold as a slave. His human flesh was bought by a king.

He worked under the whip for the goldsmith of a palace. In the heat of the flame, he spent long hours at the bellows. At night, he slept, not only weary from the day's work, but heavy with sorrow. Yet somehow, in the depths of his own despair, he found a way to lighten his spirits. One day, when no one was watching, he took a bit of gold and fashioned it into a tiny dove. Somehow, the dove reached the eyes of the King of the palace. He cried out, "Who has made this beautiful ornament? Bring the craftsman before me!"

The goldsmith came forward and admitted, "I have not made the beautiful trinket ... It was the slave, Solomon, who fashioned it."

Solomon was brought before the King and, for the first time in twelve years, he told his tale, of how he had lost his Kingship, his family, and his freedom. "Who am I?" said Solomon as he stood before the King, "without my crown, without my ring, without my family, without my freedom? Who am I? Who am I?"

The King was moved by Solomon's words and said that he would give him anything. Solomon asked only for a ship. He longed to go home.

Solomon set sail and in due time he cast his nets. When he drew them onto the deck, he saw that he had caught a fish. When he sliced open its belly he found his ring!

He slipped it onto his finger and suddenly he heard voices! People were scurrying, shouting, "King Solomon, King Solomon, wake up ... you have been asleep for an hour!"

"An hour?" he asked in disbelief.

Asmodeus, the King of the Demons, bowed low and said, "So what is real in what is seen? That which we see, that which we think we see, or something in between? If you have the answer to your question of truth and illusion, I will leave."

And Asmodeus, the King of the Demons, was gone ...

After that, Solomon became a truly wise king. He was never quick to judge. He always looked at both sides of every question, and his merciful justice was praised by all.

The Carpet, the Mirror, and the Magic Fruit

A FOLKTALE FROM THE MIDDLE EAST

*I*n a far-off time, in a far-off land, there were three princes who set out to seek their fortunes. One day, they arrived at a place where three roads forked. The oldest brother said, "Let us each go our separate ways. When the moon is full, we will return to this spot to judge who has brought the most unusual treasure."

The younger brothers agreed to the wager, and with tearful farewells, they parted. The oldest brother made his way to a great city. As he walked through the bazaar, he noticed a mysterious dark-eyed merchant displaying his wares. "Come see what I have!" cried the merchant.

When the oldest brother approached, the merchant immediately sang the praises of each item. "Here we have a bottle that never empties. Here is a bottle filled with magical waters. Drink from it and you will always be young!"

None of the wares appealed to the brother until he noticed a mirror half hidden by an embroidered scarf. As he peered into the glass, he saw the image of one of his brothers walking in a distant town. Then the image of his other brother appeared in the glass.

"What a remarkable mirror," he exclaimed. The merchant eyed his customer's fine clothing and replied, "It will cost you five thousand pieces of gold."

Without a thought, the brother emptied his purse and purchased the miraculous mirror.

Meanwhile, in a distant Bedouin camp, the next brother traveled past the tent of a weaver. Hot from his journey, the brother stopped to ask for a drink of water.

"Come in for a meal!" exclaimed the weaver. Sumptuous food was set out. As they ate, the weaver asked a thousand questions. "Where have you been? What wonders have you seen?"

The boy replied, "I have seen many strange and beautiful things in my travels, but I have not found what I am seeking. I want a truly unusual treasure to bring to my brothers when we meet again."

"Ah, yes," said the weaver, scratching his beard. "I might have just the unusual thing you seek." The weaver reached behind his cushion and drew out a small rolled-up rug. He unfurled it for the boy to see.

"It is well made," said the brother, "but it is hardly unusual."

"Ah yes," whispered the weaver, looking around to be sure that no one was listening. "But it is a magic carpet and will take you swiftly wherever you wish to go. I want only five thousand gold pieces for it."

The brother emptied his purse and bought the rug.

The third brother wandered until he came to a market where people were selling spices, fruits, and oil. As he made his way through the crowd, he saw an old beggar holding out his hand for alms. People passed quickly by him. The brother paused beside the beggar and sat down.

"How are you today, old man?" asked the boy.

"I am lonely," the man sighed. "You are the first to speak to me in many days. What brings you to this place?"

The boy replied, "I am seeking something truly unusual to bring to my brothers when we meet again."

The old man reached into his rags and pulled out a round, ripe fruit. It was a strange variety to the boy, who marveled at its beautiful color and sweet smell.

"This is no ordinary fruit," said the beggar in a hushed voice. "Its juice will cure any illness. I will sell it to you for five thousand pieces of gold."

The brother thought that surely this was the most unusual thing he would ever find. He bought it on the spot.

When the moon was full, the three brothers met again where the three roads forked. They fell joyfully into each other's arms.

"Let us judge who has brought the most unusual thing!" said the youngest brother.

"Here is a magic mirror," said the oldest. "It reveals what is happening in distant places."

The second brother displayed his carpet and boasted, "Here is a far more unusual treasure. This magic carpet will take me anywhere!"

The third brother showed his fruit and said, "The juice from this fruit can cure all illness."

"Each of us has brought interesting and unusual things," said the oldest brother. "How will we decide this wager?" As he spoke, he glanced into the mirror and saw the face of a beautiful princess. Her shining hair was black as night. Her almond-shaped eyes sparkled like deep mysterious pools. But she was weak and close to death.

The other brothers gathered around and peered into the mirror. "It is the Sultan's daughter! What a pity she is ill! Her kindness is celebrated far and wide."

"I wish I could give her this magic fruit," said the youngest brother. "Perhaps its magic would save her."

"Quickly then!" said the second brother. "Jump on my magic carpet and we will take the fruit to her bedside."

The three brothers sat on the carpet and it soared high over the desert. They traveled across the sands to the Sultan's palace and flew into the princess's room. There they saw the Sultan cradling his daughter's head, as her mother wiped her feverish brow.

Bowing low, the youngest brother spoke. "Oh great and honorable Sultan, allow me to use the magic healing powers of this strange fruit upon your daughter."

Startled by such an unusual entrance, the Sultan wiped his tears and said, "Do what you can to save her life."

The youngest brother cut the fruit in half and squeezed all of its juice into the princess's mouth. Suddenly, her cheeks flushed red, her eyes fluttered open and she sat up, as radiant as ever.

The Sultan was overjoyed! "You have saved my daughter's life with your magic fruit," he exclaimed. "Name any reward and you shall have it."

"Wait," protested the oldest brother, "it was my magic mirror which revealed where the princess lay dying!"

The second brother said, "It was my carpet which brought the magic fruit here in time!"

"Indeed," said the Sultan, "Each of you is in some way responsible for saving my daughter's life. Each of you shall receive a treasure of gold and jewels. If she wishes, I encourage my daughter to choose one of you for a husband."

The Princess sat up on her bed and eyed the brothers. "I will choose the one who has given the most to save me. This is my judgment. The magic mirror revealed my suffering, and the magic carpet brought the healing fruit to me quickly. But both the carpet and the mirror are whole and can be used again. The magic fruit has been cut and squeezed. It is spent and can no longer work its wonders. The young man who gave all of his treasure to save me gave me the gift of life. That is the greatest gift of all. I wish him for my husband."

Delighted that their wager was so wisely judged, the other two brothers stepped aside. With great joy, they celebrated the wedding of their younger brother.

May your life be as happy!

The Contest Between Wisdom and Luck

A YIDDISH FOLKTALE FROM EASTERN EUROPE

W isdom and Luck were traveling down the road together, arguing about which one of them was more important.

"Without me," said Luck, "life will always be filled with unexpected problems."

"But," said Wisdom, "if I am around, no problem is too great to solve!"

"Luck!" "Wisdom!" "Luck!" "Wisdom!"

Their argument grew heated, when suddenly, they both heard the lusty cry of a newborn babe coming from a cottage alongside the road.

Luck said, "Let's have a contest to see which of us can be more important in that young person's life as he grows. You, Wisdom, may take your turn first and I will wait until later for mine."

Wisdom agreed and leaped into the boy. The moment Wisdom entered his life, everyone around the cradle exclaimed, "This child looks wise beyond his years!"

And indeed he was! He walked and talked at an early age. When he spoke, he said remarkably intelligent things. As he grew up, he learned everything so quickly, soon no one in the village could teach him more than he already seemed to know. By the time he was a young man, he longed to see the wide world, and so he set off to seek his fortune.

He traveled until he arrived at the gates of a large city. Noticing a tailor's shop nearby, he offered himself as an apprentice. The tailor agreed to train him and was shortly amazed at how quickly the young man learned his craft. Soon the young man's garments were on display at the marketplace, and everyone

139

delighted in his beautiful designs. The King's Prime Minister noticed his handiwork and said, "You must come to the palace and be tailor to the King!"

Now, in the palace there lived a Princess who was as intelligent as she was beautiful. Although many a young prince came to court her, she found them all dull and uninteresting. She complained to her father, the King, "All the princes who come to ask for my hand in marriage are boring. I must have a husband who can engage me in interesting conversation."

"But daughter," he would say, "the Prince who came courting yesterday was rich, and the one who came today is from a fine family. You must think of your future."

"I am thinking about my future! I will not marry for wealth or high estate," she exclaimed. "I want to marry someone whose company I can enjoy. I will not speak to any more of them! I will seal my lips and remain silent until a suitor comes who says something which will make me want to respond."

And from that moment on, the Princess would speak to no one.

The King was furious at her stubbornness and announced, "I will give the Princess's hand in marriage to any man, be he of royalty or peasantry, who can make her speak." To avoid frivolous suitors, he also announced, "Anyone who tries and fails will be put to death."

Many young men tried. Many young men died. The Princess remained silent and content in her solitude.

One day, as the young tailor was stitching the King's hem in the royal chamber, he happened to see the Princess walk past the door. He thought, "If she is as intelligent as she is beautiful, we would make a fine match."

As the young man fitted the King with an elegant suit of clothes he said, "I would like a chance to try and encourage the Princess to speak."

"It will be a pity," said the King, "to lose such a fine tailor. If you fail you will die."

"Fear not," said the lad, "I will not fail, for I am wise beyond my years."

"Guard!" called the King, "take this arrogant young man to the Princess's chamber. If she speaks to him, inform me immediately. If she does not speak … hang him!"

A guard led the lad to the Princess's chamber and stationed himself outside the door. "Listen carefully at the keyhole," said the tailor as he entered the Princess's chamber, closing the door behind him.

Being a young man who was indeed wise beyond his years, the tailor did not speak to the Princess. Instead, he turned to the candelabrum burning bright with candles and began a story.

> *Candelabrum, candelabrum, I've a tale to tell.*
> *Candelabrum, candelabrum, listen, listen well ...*

Long ago, three wise men rode through a dark forest. At nightfall, they camped and made a fire. Fearful of wild beasts in the night, they each agreed to take turns standing guard until the dawn.

The first man to stand guard was an excellent carpenter. To pass the time, he took out his whittling knife and carved a beautiful maiden out of a log. Then he woke the second wise man and went to sleep.

The second man was an excellent tailor. When the tailor saw the beautiful maiden of wood he said to himself, " 'Tis a pity that such a lovely girl does not have a gown and cloak to clothe her." He took some cloth from his pack and he snipped and stitched until he had sewn her a fine gown and cloak. Then he woke the third wise man and went to sleep.

The third man was an excellent teacher. When the teacher saw the beautiful maiden with the fine gown and cloak he thought, " 'Tis a pity she cannot speak." He patiently set about to teach her to talk. So magical were his skills, that before long she sat up, and they gaily spoke with each other until dawn.

When the other two men awoke and saw the maiden, they each insisted that she ride with them.

"I carved her," said the carpenter, "I deserve her company most."

"But I clothed her!" said the tailor, "She should ride with me!"

"But I gave her the gift of speech," said the teacher, "and so she can speak for herself. With which of us, dear lady, would you like to ride?"

"Candelabrum," said the young man, "which one do YOU think she chose, the one who carved her, the one who clothed her, or the one who gave her the gift of speech?

"Speak up, candelabrum!" the young man insisted, "Guess which one ..."

Well, of course the candelabrum couldn't talk! But the Princess, who had been listening to the story the whole time, blurted out, "She should go with the one who gave her the choice ..."

The lad whirled about and said to the Princess, who gasped at hearing her own voice, "Aha! I have won you fairly! You spoke! And if you would have me for a husband I would gladly have you for my bride."

The Princess blushed and agreed to the wedding.

The lad dashed out the door to tell the King. But as he passed the guard, the huge man grabbed him by the shirt collar and bellowed, "I am taking you to your death, young man! You have failed."

The young man protested, "I have not failed! She spoke! She spoke! Didn't you hear?"

Although the boy had great wisdom, he did not have luck. And as luck would have it, the guard had been asleep the whole time and heard nothing but his own snoring.

Luck and Wisdom were observing the young man's predicament. Luck said smugly to Wisdom, "Look what you've done! That young man is indeed wise beyond his years, but he shall lose his life in moments unless I step in now."

Luck jumped into the body of the young man just as the guard was dragging him to the gallows which loomed in front of the Princess's balcony. And as luck would have it, she happened to walk outside at the same moment. When the Princess saw what was happening she cried out, "Stop! Set him free! That man is to be my husband. He will tell me stories!"

And so the tailor and the Princess were joyously married. Luck and Wisdom attended the celebration, and the minstrels sang a wedding blessing,

> *"May your home be filled with wisdom,*
> *May your love always be true,*
> *As you weave your lives together,*
> *May luck be with you!"*

And they lived happily, wisely, and luckily ever after ....

Notes

THE MAGIC BROCADE (CHINA), P. 11

My retelling of "The Magic Brocade" is based on a popular folktale of the Chuang people from the Kwangsi Province of southern China. The Chuang culture is ancient, dating back over two thousand years. Chuang artists have long been noted for their exquisite silk brocade weaving, their fine painting and design. This folktale celebrates both the art of the region and the filial love and devotion a son shows his mother. Other printed versions are included in:

The Magic Boat and other Chinese Folk Stories by M.A. Jagendorf (New York: The Vanguard Press Inc., 1980).
The Spring of Butterflies and other Chinese Folktales by He Liyi (New York: Lothrop, Lee and Shepard Books, 1985).
Folk and Fairytales of Far Off Lands by Eric Potter (JCA Literary Agency, 1965).

THE TALKING SKULL (WEST AFRICA), P. 17

"The Talking Skull" is a story about talking. It is a popular cautionary tale told by storytellers in many parts of Africa. My retelling adds a touch of poetry but clings essentially to the plot line. Commentary about the Nigerian version can be found in *African Folktales: Selected and Retold* by Roger D. Abraham (New York: Pantheon Books, 1983). Another printed version of "The Talking Skull" can be found as "Now You Know" in Loreto Todd's book, *The Tortoise and Other Trickster Tales From Cameroon* (New York: Schocken Books, 1979).

THE MAGIC MILL (NORWAY), P. 21

My retelling of "The Magic Mill" is based on the folktale "How the Sea Became Salt," collected in Norway by Peter Christen Absjörnsen and Jörgen Moe and first published in 1845 in their book, *Norwegian Folk Tales*. Inspired by the work of the Brothers Grimm in Germany, Absjörnsen and Moe set about to preserve the rich folkloric tradition of Norway. The Norwegian folktales they collected reflect the rural lifestyle of the storytellers themselves. Tales were told around the hearth during the long winter evenings by both men and women tellers, who were highly esteemed in their communities. Contemporary print translations are included in:

Norwegian Folk Tales by Peter Christian Absjörnsen and Moe Jörgen (New York: Pantheon Books, 1982).

Blue Fairy Book by Andrew Lang (England: Longmans, Green Co. Ltd., 1889).

True and Untrue and Other Norse Tales by Sigrid Undset (New York: Alfred A. Knopf, 1962).

THE BLIZZARD WITCH OF THE NORTH (SIBERIAN ARCTIC), P. 25

"The Blizzard Witch of the North" is based on a Siberian folktale entitled "Bold Yatto and His Sister Tayune." The tale was collected by James Riordan during his journey to the far north of Siberia where he lived with native people. It appears in his book, *The Sun Maiden and The Crescent Moon* (New York: Interlink Publishing Group, 1989). Mr. Riordan's collection has helped to preserve one of the few remaining oral traditions that has not been eroded by modern technology. Living for months in Arctic dwellings, Mr. Riordan heard tales told as they have been shared for an eon around the hearth fires of the cold north.

URASHIMA THE FISHERMAN (JAPAN), P. 31

Tales featuring a supernatural passage of time have delighted listeners in many cultures, from the New England tale of Rip Van Winkle to the Jewish story of the bridegroom, who visits the grave of a friend on his wedding night and, after what seems to be but a few hours, returns many years later. "Urashima, the Fisherman" is a well-known Japanese folktale that incorporates this theme of suspended time. My retelling of the tale is based on a version collected by the American reporter, Lafcadio Hearn, who went to Japan in the late 1800's and published a collection entitled, *Japanese Fairytales,* with T. Hasegawa and Son, Tokyo. Contemporary versions in print are included in:

The Boy Who Drew Cats and Other Tales by Lafcadio Hearn (New York: MacMillan, 1963).

Japanese Fairy Tales by Lafcadio Hearn (New York: Liveright Publishing Corporation, 1953).

Japanese Tales by Royall Tyler (New York: Pantheon Books, 1987).

MOTHER HOLLE (GERMANY), P. 35

My retelling of "Mother Holle" is based on a story collected by Wilhelm and Jacob Grimm for their landmark book, *The Household Tales*. In the early 1800s these two philologists collected word phrases and expressions they feared were being lost as the agricultural population of the countryside swept off to live in the cities during the early days of industrialization. Beyond such colloquial phrases, however, these two students of language found a wealth of "märchen" or household tales, now preserved in countless anthologies through their archival efforts. The tale of "Mother Holle" was collected in 1812 from Wilhelm Grimm's bride, Dortchen Wild, of Kassel. Translated versions can be found in:

Household Tales From the Collection of the Brothers Grimm by Lucy Crane (London: Macmillan & Co., 1882).

The Complete Grimm's Fairy Tales by Padric Colum (New York: Pantheon Books, 1944).

The Complete Fairy Tales of the Brothers Grimm by Jack Zipes (New York: Bantam Books, 1987).

THE SEALSKIN (ICELAND), P. 41

My fascination with tales of silkies began with my own singing, as a youngster, of the Childe folk ballad, "Silkie of Skule Skerry," which celebrates this shape shifter. Tales of ill-fated love between seals and humans abound along the coasts of Scotland and Iceland. My retelling of "The Sealskin" is based a version from *Icelandic Folktales and Legends* by Jacqueline Simpson (University of California Press, 1972). A Scottish version can be found in:

Animal Folktales Around the World by Kathleen Arnott (New York: Walck, 1971).

THE TIGER, THE BRAHMAN, AND THE JACKAL (INDIA), P. 45

Fables, stories in which animals talk and act like people, abound in oral traditions throughout the world. In this thought provoking, ancient story of injustice and a world alive with talking things, non-animal characters, such as the road and the tree, speak too. Jackal, the trickster in this tale, is a playful character, and so I have portrayed him speaking in rhymes. This tale is derivative of the story of the "Genie in the Bottle" from *The Tales of the Arabian Nights*. A powerful demon or creature is caged or bottled and is coaxed, through wit, back into captivity. Variations of this plot exist in both Europe and Africa. In an American Appalachian Mountain version, a snake is similarly coaxed back into a trap by Br'er Fox.

Other print versions of "The Tiger, the Brahman, and the Jackal" can be found in:

Favorite Fairy Tales Told In India, by Virginia Haviland (Boston: Little Brown & Co., 1973).

Indian Fairy Tales, by Joseph Jacobs (New York/London: Putnam, 1892).

WILEY AND THE HAIRY MAN (UNITED STATES), P. 51

This popular southern folktale was collected in the 1930s for the Federal Writers Project of the Works Progress Administration of the State of Alabama by Donnell Van de Voort. The tale features a strong heroine and a roguish son who outwit a devilish conjure man. A reference to a giraffe, which is not an indigenous animal, suggests that the story was brought by African captives. Van de Voort's WPA transcription in dialect can be found at the Library of Congress in Washington, D.C. and in *A Treasury of American Folklore: Stories, Ballads, and Traditions of the People,* edited by B.A. Botkin (New York: Crown Publishers, 1944). A contemporary edited version can be found in Virginia Haviland's *North American Legends* (New York: William Collins Publishers, 1979).

THE GOLDEN GOOSE (GERMANY), P. 55

This retelling of "The Golden Goose" is based on a well known folktale collected in 1812 by the Brothers Grimm in Germany for their publication of "märchen" or household tales. The tale was gathered from the Hassenpflugs, a family with Huguenot roots who lived in Kassel. The goose in the plot is an ancient element with origins in a Jataka tale from India. Printed versions can be found in:

The Complete Grimm's Fairy Tales by Padric Colum (New York: Pantheon Books, 1944).

Household Tales From the Collection of the Brothers Grimm by Lucy Crane (London: Macmillan & Co., 1882).

The Complete Fairy Tales of the Brothers Grimm by Jack Zipes (New York: Bantam Books, 1987).

THE MAGIC OYSTERS OF THE QUEEN OF THE SOUTH SEA (INDONESIA), P. 61

Indonesia is an archipelago of one thousand islands. Lush and tropical, it is a country with many diverse cultural influences. Long before the Moslem religion became dominant, travelers from India brought Hinduism and then Buddhism. Indigenous peoples worshiped the natural world around them. "The Magic Oysters of the Queen of the South Sea" is based on an ancient folktale with animistic imagery collected in Indonesia by Adele De Leeuw and printed in her book, *Indonesian Legends and Folk Tales* (New York: Thomas Nelson & Sons, 1964).

While visiting Indonesia I heard many legends and superstitions about the Queen of the South Sea. "Never wear a green bathing suit," I was warned. Legend has it that a princess long ago dropped her green weaving thread into the ocean. She jumped in after it and drowned. Her ghost has everafter been reaching for the green thread she lost. The strong undertow in places is thought to be the Queen of the South Sea reaching for her thread. Woe to anyone wearing that color in the sea, for the Queen will reach out and drag them under!

THE SAD STORY OF STONE FROGS (ABORIGINAL, AUSTRALIA), P. 67

This story was collected by British author K. Langloh Parker, who grew up in Australia and lived among Aboriginal people. She first published her collection in London in 1896. The collection was welcomed as a folklore classic, sensitively reflecting in story a culture that was quickly disappearing. The tale I chose to retell from the collection, as well as other myths and legends offering insights into aboriginal lifestyle, can be found in her book, *Australian Legendary Tales* (New York: Viking Press, 1966).

TALK! TALK! (ASHANTI, WEST AFRICA), P. 71

To keep the listener's attention, the griot, or storyteller, in an African village setting might weave a rhythmic song into the communal telling to invite the listeners to join in with the tale. In my retelling of this tale I have suggested the audience participation by adding a repeated refrain.

This folktale plot, where talking things surprise human listeners, originated in West Africa. It traveled with slaves to the New World, and related variations of it have been documented in African-American folklore. Other printed versions of this tale include:

Afro-American Folktales by Roger D. Abrahams (New York: Pantheon Books, 1985).

The Things That Talked: Folklore of the Antilles by Elsie Clews Parsons (New York: American Folklore Society, 1943).

The Cow Tale Switch and Other West African Stories by Harold Courlander and George Herzog (New York: Henry Holt & Co., 1947).

THE MAN WHO COULD TRANSFORM HIMSELF (KENYA), P. 75

The transformation of the pursuer and the pursued into different animal forms during a chase is an ancient magical theme. My version of "The Man Who Could Transform Himself" is based on an Akamba tale from Kenya, Africa. Other variations, according to noted folklore scholar Indries Shah in his notes for *World Tales*, can be found in *1001 Arabian Nights,* in the collections by the Brothers Grimm, in the Welsh story cycle *The Mabinogion,* and in the *Siddhi Kur*, a Buddhist collection of legends. See also:

African Folktales by Roger D. Abrahams (New York: Pantheon Books, 1983).

Akamba Stories by John S. Mbiti (Oxford: Oxford University Press, 1966).

"A Contest of Magicians," from *World Tales* by Indries Shah (New York: Harcourt Brace Jovanovich, 1979).

DUFFY AND THE DEVIL (ENGLAND), P. 79

Guessing the name of an evil character to free oneself from the powers of its wickedness is a theme which appears in numerous European folktales. Variants include the well-known "Rumpelstiltskin," the English tale "Tom Tit Tot," and the Scottish version, "Whuppity Stoorie." My retelling of "Duffy and the Devil" is based on "Duffy and the Devil Terrytop," as collected by Robert Hunt in his book *Popular Romances of the West of England* (New York/London: Benjamin Blom Publishers, 1916) and from a droll based on the tale entitled "Lady Lovel's Courtship," a popular play often performed in olden days during the Christmas season in Cornwall, England.

THE GOLDEN TOUCH (ANCIENT GREECE), P. 85

This tale was told in Greece by ancient bards long before it was written by the Roman poet Ovid, who lived in the first century A.D. This story is a fragment of the huge body of Greek myths which flourished through the oral tradition before there was a written Greek language. Retold again and again, this ancient tale can be found in many modern versions including one by Nathaniel Hawthorne, who added the character of the daughter who is turned to gold, a detail ever since perpetuated by contemporary storytellers. Other sources of Greek myths with print versions of this tale include:

Book of Greek Myths by Ingri and Edgar D'Aulaire (Garden City, New York: Doubleday, 1962).

Mythology: Timeless Tales of Gods and Heroes by Edith Hamilton (New York: Little Brown and Co., 1942).

THE CONTRARY FAIRY (FRENCH CANADA), P. 89

This folktale was collected in French Canada by renowned North American folk-lorist Marius Barbeau, who was anthropologist to the National Museum of Canada. The story is reminiscent of classical French folktales found in Charles Perrault's *Histoires et Contes de Temps Passé,* otherwise known as *Mother Goose Tales,* which was first published in English in 1697. Overtones of "Sleeping Beauty" abound, with birthday visits from a good fairy who gives a blessing and an evil fairy who gives a curse. There is a prison of rose briar thorns and a happy wedding at the end for a Prince and Princess. Through songs, and especially storytelling, the French Canadian colonists preserved their French heritage. Marius Barbeau's version of this tale, "The Fairy Quite Contrary," can be found in *The Golden Phoenix: Eight French Canadian Fairy Tales* (New York: Henry Z. Walck, Inc., 1958).

DRAKESTAIL (FRANCE), P. 97

This old French folktale is a political satire. Since ancient times, storytellers have used the form of the fable to comment on the politics of their time. Animals who talk and act like people can safely criticize or poke fun at a ruler where such complaint by an individual might be dangerous. I suspect that the story of Drakestail was born in this manner.

Other printed versions can be found in:

Best-Loved Folktales of the World by Joanna Cole (New York: Doubleday, 1983).
The Wonder Story Books: It Happened One Day by Miriam Huber and Mabel O'Donnell (New York: Harper and Row, 1976).

THE MOUSE BRIDE (FINLAND), P. 101

This tale of enchantment celebrates the ancient and recurring theme of true love in spite of beastly appearance. Versions abound in cultures around the globe, the most well known being the French tale of "Beauty and the Beast" and the Norwegian tale of "East o' the Moon and West o' the Sun." My retelling of "The Mouse Bride" is based on a popular Finnish folktale. See also:

Tales From a Finnish Tupa by James Cloyd Bowman and Margery Bianco (Chicago: Albert Whitman & Co., 1964).
"The Forest Bride" from *The Shepherd's Nosegay* by Fillmore Parker (New York: Harcourt Brace & World Inc., 1958).

THE PEDLAR OF SWAFFHAM (ENGLAND), P. 109

My version of this tale is based on the legend of John Chapman as told by Joseph Jacobs in his book, *More English Fairytales,* originally published in 1894. The Swaffham Church in Norfolk has a statue of Chapman, carved in 1462, with the inscription, "Pray for the health of John Chapman and his wife and children, which John caused this aisle to be made with windows and roof."

This legend has ancient parallels in a tale from *1001 Arabian Nights,* which features a young spendthrift from Baghdad whose dream sends him to Cairo and back home again to find a buried treasure. A Jewish version of the tale was told in the villages of Poland and is retold by Uri Shulevitz in his picture book, *The Treasure.* Contemporary print versions of "The Pedlar of Swaffham" can be found in:

More English Fairy Tales by Joseph Jacobs (New York: Dover Publications, 1967).
Round the World Fairy Tales by Anabel Williams-Ellis (London/Glasgow: Blackie, 1963).

THE BOY WHO DREW CATS (JAPAN), P. 113

Supernatural tales in which an artist's genius at capturing reality allows their artwork to come to life are common in both Chinese and Japanese folklore. My retelling of "The Boy Who Drew Cats" is based on an old legend from Japan about the 15th century artist Sesshu Toyo, whose ink drawings of animals were so lifelike they seemed to move. A version of the tale was collected by the American reporter, Lafcadio Hearn, in the late 1800s and published in his book *Japanese Fairy Tales* (Tokyo: T. Hasegawa and Son). A contemporary print version can be found in:

Japanese Fairy Tales by Lafcadio Hearn (New York: Liveright Publishing Corporation, 1953).
The Boy Who Drew Cats and Other Tales by Lafcadio Hearn (New York: MacMillan, 1963).

THE SEARCH FOR THE MAGIC LAKE (ECUADOR), P. 117

When the Spanish conquistador Francisco Pizarro captured the great Inca ruler Atahualpa in 1532, Atahualpa suggested his own ransom. He offered to command his people to fill his prison cell with golden objects. To Pizarro, this was an enormous fortune. To Inca people, however, gold was used for decoration, not money.

Caravans of llamas loaded with golden objects began arriving at the prison. Golden statues, utensils, flasks, and sheets of gold, stripped from temple walls, filled the cell. Caravans of gold were still coming when Pizarro executed Atahualpa anyway.

This treachery outraged the Incas carrying gold to the prison. They tormented the Spanish soldiers by hiding golden objects deep in caves and in lakes, far out of the reach of greedy hands. One of these golden objects which did not reach its destination was the golden flask filled with healing water from the Magic Lake. Decades of Inca rulers had preserved the magic golden flask. Now all that remains of the flask is this story, which is still told in Ecuador today.

My retelling of "The Search For The Magic Lake" is based on a version collected by Genevieve Barlow in Quito, Ecuador, between 1938 and 1964. It appears in the collection *Latin American Tales: From the Pampas to the Pyramids of Mexico* (New York: Rand McNally & Company, 1966).

THE OLDEN GOLDEN GOOSE (A JATAKA TALE FROM INDIA), P. 123

Jataka tales are an ancient Indian cycle of stories featuring the Buddha in many incarnations. The golden feathered goose from this old plot reappears in the more contemporary version of "The Golden Goose," collected with expansive plot development in Germany by the Brothers Grimm. Other print versions of this tale can be found in:

More Jataka Tales by Ellen C. Babbitt (New York: The Century Co., 1922).
The Hungry Tigress by Rafe Martin (Berkeley, California: Parallax Press, 1990).

THE FIREBIRD, THE HORSE OF POWER, AND THE PRINCESS VASILISSA (RUSSIA), P. 125

There are several tales in the oral tradition of Russia which feature the names of the characters in this story. The Firebird, a much sought-after bird with fiery golden feathers, is likely derived from the Phoenix, a supernatural bird from the mythology of both Egypt and China. According to legend, the ancient Phoenix lives for five hundred years at a time, builds its own funeral pyre, is consumed in the flames, and then resurrects itself from its own ashes as a fiery feathered bird.

"The Firebird, the Horse of Power, and the Princess Vasilissa" is a popular Russian folktale plot which I have chosen to include because of its strong and resourceful heroine. Versions of the story appear in several classic collections of Russian stories:

Russian Fairy Tales by Aleksandr Afanas'ev (New York: Pantheon Books, 1973).
Old Peter's Russian Tales by Arthur Ransome (London: Thomas Nelson & Sons, 1916).

THE BEGGAR KING (A KING SOLOMON TALE FROM BABYLONIA), P. 131

To prevent Asmodeus, the Demon King, from stopping the construction of the holy temple, King Solomon captured Asmodeus and imprisoned him in a dungeon. The tale of "The Beggar King" takes place upon the completion of the temple, when Asmodeus is about to be set free. This tale is one of many stories from the Jewish tradition which center on the wisdom of King Solomon. Special thanks to Howard Schwartz for bringing this story to light for me in his book, *Elijah's Violin and Other Jewish Fairy Tales* (New York: Harper and Row Publishers, 1983). Another printed version can be found in:

> *Legends of the Bible* by Louis Ginzberg (Philadelphia: The Jewish Publication Society of America, 1975).

THE CARPET, THE MIRROR, AND THE MAGIC FRUIT (MIDDLE EAST), P. 135

Versions of "The Carpet, the Mirror, and the Magic Fruit" appear in numerous Middle Eastern areas including Israel, Morocco, Libya, Tunisia, Egypt and Yemen. Several Jewish variants are filed in the Israel Folktale Archive. The type of fruit varies from apple to citrus, depending upon the source of the variant. Other printed versions of this story can be found as:

> "Who Cured the Princess?" from *Folktales of Israel* by Dov Noy (Chicago: The University of Chicago Press, 1963).
>
> "The Magic Pomegranate," from *Jewish Stories One Generation Tells Another* by Peninnah Schram (Northvale, New Jersey: Jason Aronson Inc., 1987).
>
> "A Mirror, a Carpet and a Lemon," from *A Treasury of Turkish Folktales for Children* by Barbara K. Walker (Connecticut: Linnet Books, 1988).

THE CONTEST BETWEEN WISDOM AND LUCK
(A YIDDISH FOLKTALE FROM EASTERN EUROPE), P. 139

My retelling of "The Contest between Wisdom and Luck" is inspired by a Yiddish tale collected in 1928 by folklorist Y.L. Cahan, from storyteller Rokhl Rabin in Orinin, U.S.S.R. It was first published in Cahan's book, Yidishe Folksmayses, and can currently be found in Yiddish at YIVO Institute for Jewish Research, New York, and in Beatrice Weinrich's anthology, Yiddish Folktales (New York: Pantheon Books, 1988).

During the decades before World War I many Jewish "zamlers," or folklorists, carefully documented the rich oral tradition of the Yiddish communities in Eastern Europe (Russia to the east, Poland to the west, Latvia to the north and Romania to the south) and deposited folklore, folktales, holiday customs, proverbs, parables and allegories at The Yiddish Research Institute, YIVO, in Vilna, Poland.

During the German occupation of Vilna in 1941, many of the countless tales collected for the YIVO archives were destroyed. But after the war, Allied officers discovered 50,000 manuscripts and 30,000 archival folders at the Nazis' Institute for Research on the Jewish Question in Frankfurt. In 1948, this treasury of Yiddish oral lore was sent, in wooden crates, to the YIVO Institute in New York where scholarly preservation is continuing to this day.

My special thanks to editor Beatrice Weinrich, who brought this story to light for me in her book, *Yiddish Folktales;* to the librarians at YIVO, New York, from whom I obtained the original Yiddish version; and to Esther Newman, who translated this tale out loud over tea, allowing me to hear it in the "mame-loshn" (mother tongue).

SPECIAL THANKS TO:

Dinah Foglia, Robert Friedman, Laurel Foglia, Lucas Foglia, Lawrence Foglia, Rita Auerbach, Susan Gaber, Nancy Yost, and Rufus Griscom for their encouragement and careful reading of this book as it grew.